EUPHORIA
A REVERSE HAREM FANTASY ROMANCE

DEVYN SINCLAIR

Copyright © 2019 Devyn Sinclair

All rights reserved.

No part of this book may be reproduced in any form or by any electronic or mechanical means, including information storage and retrieval systems, without written permission from the author, except for the use of brief quotations in a book review. No part of this book may be used to create, feed, or refine artificial intelligence models, for any purpose, without written permission from the author.

❦ Created with Vellum

CHAPTER ONE

KARI

There's warmth in this darkness, and the barest sensation of touch. It tingles and soothes and arouses. Is that magic too? But it's not magic I know. It's blue, with strength like the wind and the taste of the ocean. That sensation of opening your eyes underwater and seeing nothing but the infinite. It feels *good*. But I can't move, can't speak. Not with my mouth at least. *Who are you?*

The reflection comes back to me deeper. *Who are you?*

A brush of lips on mine, and pulling away. The presence is leaving, and I don't want them to go. *Wait.*

But they don't stop, leaving me alone. I think I feel a tinge of regret, but that's all as I'm abandoned in the warm dark. There's a sound that's far more sinister, the slicing of metal, and fear slithers in my chest. Where is that? What's there?

Again, and louder, the sound of death and fear. No. Please, not again. I just want to be safe. Not again.

The sounds of battle rouse me from sleep, and I sit up, heart pounding, the clatter I heard fading into nothing. My room around me is peaceful, and I ease back down onto the pillows, taking a breath to make my pulse chill the fuck out. The sound of steel on steel rings out again, along with a curse.

They're training again.

I don't suppose they're going to stop at all. After the intruder they decided to start daily training, all to keep me safe. It's only been a couple days, and I can't help but still be nervous when I'm out in the grounds. The fae men swear by the wards they've put in place, and I can see them pulsing with shimmering color if I manage to make it all the way to the walls. But I still keep seeing it in my mind: the way that fae looked at me with pure, fiery hatred, and chose to kill me rather than just leave with his mission failed.

And he's my mate. I can't forget that fact. I haven't told anyone else, either. I don't imagine the rest of my mates are going to take kindly to *that* little fact.

I roll over, pulling the blanket over my head. I want to go back to sleep, but my heart is still pounding with residual adrenaline, and my stomach is starting to wake up too. Soon the smell of breakfast food will be tempting enough to make me get up. I've learned this.

One benefit of living in this house is that it knows what I love. And my bedroom is basically my favorite place in the sprawling mansion. It's spacious—by far the biggest of the bedrooms, with a bed that would be almost the size of my studio apartment in New York. Which makes me giggle every time I think about it, because the house clearly knows what I need it for: sharing.

There's a fountain and bathing pool in one area, the pool cascading into a series of fountains that lead out into the gardens. There are books and ingredients for potions if I ever want to make them again, and the closet that's literally stuffed full of clothes—half of them sent from Kaya, and the rest formed from the magic of the house reading my subconscious. Everything is perfect and gorgeous and I can't believe that it's real. How can any of it be real?

Of course, things are less perfect when you consider the homicidal fae female who's trying to kill me. But I'm trying not to think about that.

I shove the blanket off my head again, listening to the soft sounds of scuffling coming from outside. There's a robe on the floor from where I dropped it last night—it's quickly become one of my favorites. Soft and fluffy and fitted enough that it doesn't make me feel like I'm drowning. I slip it on over the little nightgown I wore to sleep. When I went to sleep I was wrapped in warm arms and soft kisses and I'd rather have woken up to that. At the same time, the fact that they're dedicated to protecting me is something that I'm still overwhelmed by.

Trying to be quiet, I sneak out of my bedroom so I can see the four of them in the courtyard below. I get a waft of scent from the garden, and I breathe it in. Surrounded by flowers and plants as we are, everything smells *amazing*. Some of the books in my room are guides to Allwyn plants and herbology books that I want to take the time to read. If I ever go back to the shop, the knowledge will be helpful.

Leaning against one of the pillars, I peer down into the courtyard. Brae, Aeric, Kent, and Urien stand off in pairs against each other. They've conveniently lost their shirts—which I don't mind in the slightest—and are covered in a sheen of sweat. Verys is still recovering. He's barely been conscious over the last two days, and I've spent time with him as much as I've been able. Urien assures me that he'll be okay, but I don't like seeing him like this.

Even with Verys in recovery, the last few days have been lovely. We've taken things slow and gotten to know each other. I told the rest of the fae males about my history as a dancer, and the fall and events after it that ended my career. I've learned a little more about each of them as well, though it's not enough. I want to know everything. And for the first time since I've met them it seems like I'll actually have the *time* to get to know them.

Below me, Aeric lunges at Kent with the knife that he's holding. It's impossibly fast—an absolute blur. I gasp as Kent seems to blur too, dodging to the side and attempting to knock the knife from Aeric's hand and failing. They grapple, Kent breaking free and stepping back. But he doesn't stop moving, seeming to climb up Aeric's body and swing his legs with a momentum that flips Aeric flat on the ground and leaves Kent in control.

"Fuck," Aeric says as Kent lets him go. "Still didn't see it coming."

"I'll teach it to you tomorrow," Kent says, no shortage of smugness on his face.

Aeric springs to his feet from flat on his back like the movement is nothing. It's been a long time since I could move with that kind of athletic power, and watching the ease of his movement makes me want to get back to that place. "Why tomorrow?" He asks.

"Because I need a few more times that I can actually kick your ass."

All of them laugh, and I can't keep the smile off my face. I like watching them together, and I like that Kent is getting along with them. That they've accepted him even though he's not fae. Then again, neither am I.

Urien notices me watching and winks. Three other faces turn and look up at me, and now my heart is pounding for an entirely different reason. I can't seem to wrap my head around the fact that these men want me. Unequivocally and without reservation. Every time they do something like that my brain slams on the brakes and tells me no fucking way that this is the truth. But the way they're looking at me makes my stomach flutter, and I don't have any doubts about the rightness of it, even if it still blows my mind.

"Morning," Kent says.

"Morning." I'm blushing because I can't keep the silly smile off my face.

"We're just finishing," Brae says. "Join us?"

"Whatever for?" I say, teasing. Of course I want to join them. For anything. For everything. I walk down the sweeping staircase to find them waiting for me. Brae takes my hand and pulls me against his body. He's hot from the training, glistening with sweat. Kent steps up behind me, giving me a hug and a kiss on the neck while Brae takes my lips.

Oh *yes*.

Goddess, he can kiss. Teasing my lips open with

his own and tracing my tongue, tantalizing me with sunny magic that tastes like honey and makes me forget all about my plans for breakfast.

I'm dazed when he pulls away, and speechless for anything to do with his kiss or the way their bodies are pressed against mine. Heat and work and sweat. "I'm going to have to wash this robe now," I say.

"The house will do it for you," Urien says. "But let's not make it any dirtier." He pushes the robe off my shoulders, and I laugh as it drops to the floor.

"It really is too bad that we're dirty," Kent says. "We should clean up." He sweeps me off my feet without warning, carrying me through the house to the bath. The huge room has a glass ceiling and pools of different shapes, sizes, and temperatures. All big enough to fit more than one person, of course. I can practically hear the magic in the house laughing in delight.

The air is thick with steam from the hot pools, haze floating skyward in lazy shapes from the perfect crystal water. It's equally magnificent in here at night, the magic infused in the water glowing like some of those caves you see in the human world. The more I think about it the more I think this might also be one of my favorite rooms in the house —despite the fact that my own private bath is glorious.

Kent walks straight into the largest pool, which is warm and steaming. The water sinks through the thin nightgown and my hair as we go deeper. But it feels delicious, like curling up in a blanket. A blanket that has arms like steel.

The other men are behind us, already naked as they enter the water. Already hard. "Sneaky," I say. "Thought you'd kill two birds with one stone?"

Aeric pulls me out of Kent's arms and onto his lap, sitting on one of the low benches in the water. "We're training hard to protect you," he says, grinning. "Don't you think we deserve a reward?"

He kisses me hard, only breaking away to pull the soaked nightgown over my head and toss it away before crushing my mouth to his again. Reaching between us, he teases me with his fingers. He's taunting me because he knows that I know what he can do with his mouth—and that I love it.

The past couple of days we've held back, because I'm still recovering and they don't want to force me too fast. We've kissed plenty, and they've made me come, but nothing more. Even now, even though I'm pressing my hips towards him and rubbing against his cock, Aeric is unmoved, teasing me and kissing me like he has no other care in the world.

"You don't have to earn fucking me," I tell him. "Any time. Right now, actually, would be good."

Aeric bites down on my lip, pulling me back into the kiss. A moan escapes me as he adds magic to his fingers, stroking me deeper and making me shudder in pleasure. His power curls into me, twisting into the places that make me tremble, tipping me over the edge faster than I thought possible.

The orgasm gathers at my core, and sharp, sudden pleasure rolls through me. I let my forehead fall against his shoulder, shaking with need, his clever fingers still stroking until I can barely breathe. Fuck, I want more of him. I want the fullness that accompanies his cock. I've felt it before and I want it again, but I can't speak through the shaking of my body.

New hands skim my waist, pulling me away from Aeric, and he lets me go, that fierce hungry look in his eyes that tells me he wants to devour me. I can see his hand moving under the water, seeing to his own pleasure.

Kent holds me against his chest, arms wrapped firmly around me. His cock is nestled perfectly against my ass, and I want it. I squirm, trying to get him to give in, but he doesn't. Instead a finger slips inside my pussy, and then two. My eyes roll back, taking my head with it. Fuck. Damn it all.

I'm biting my lip, trying to keep myself from crying out. His fingers curl up into me, brushing my

G-spot, and thrusting against it. My body is ready for it, pleasure exploding behind my eyes in a blinding flash. I jerk against Kent's body but his arm keeps me anchored to him.

"Damn you," I say, my voice slipping out. "You're too good at that."

He chuckles, lips tickling my ear. "That's a compliment I'll take any day."

Urien lifts me out of the water with ease, spreading me on the tile beside the pool. It's warm and wet, and the scent of water fills the space around me. "I haven't tasted you yet," he says softly. His fingers are on my thighs and then his tongue is on me and he makes a sound like a starving man as he consumes me.

Brae kisses my lips again, hand stroking my hair. His tongue invades my mouth, stroking, dancing, teasing. Such different rhythms with each tongue, and yet they work in harmony, driving me up and over the cliff and letting me fall into pleasure twice before either of them stop.

I can't catch my breath as Brae pulls away, his eyes shining with amusement. Urien's mouth is shining with me, and he licks his lips, sending a fresh burst of arousal straight to my clit. "The perfect appetizer," he says. "For breakfast."

Brae helps me off the stone and picks me up this

time, not even commenting on the fact that my skin is shimmering faintly, glowing with the remnants of their magic. He holds me close as we walk out of the bath. They've made a habit of this, picking me up and carrying me. Like they used to have to do when I couldn't walk. I haven't told them to stop, because I like it when they hold me.

"Wait," I say. "None of you…" I freeze. I'm still not used to saying things like this out loud. "None of you came."

"It's not always about that," Aeric says.

"I'm fine," I say. "I'm not going to break."

Brae pulls me a little closer. "We know. But this is new for everyone. And now we have the luxury of taking a little time to see how it works, not being forced into extremes because you need the magic." There's a moment of tension in the air, none of us quite ready to think about the fact everything almost went very differently, and I almost wasn't here. Brae speaks again, "Besides, I like hearing the sounds you make when you come."

There's general sounds of agreement as he walks me into the common room, where the dining table has breakfast laid out. I hadn't thought that maybe it was as shocking for them as it is for me. They have all seemed very much okay with it, like they fell into it naturally. But this has to be strange for them too.

"Yeah," I say quietly. "You don't have to carry me everywhere."

"I enjoy having you naked and in my arms," Brae says simply, before he kisses my forehead and puts me down near the table. One thing that definitely doesn't seem to bother them is the nudity. I'm not used to it, and I have the urge to cover myself even though they were all just touching me. Had their hands and mouths on me and in me.

I cross my arms over my chest. "Look," I say. "I know this is different, and I'm not really sure we all know how it works. But please don't hold back. When I said that I wanted all of you, I meant it. In every sense. Unless you've changed your minds."

"Never," Aeric says. There's pure conviction in his voice, gaze fierce on mine.

The rest of them shake their heads, confirming that this is what they want. But there are a lot of things to talk about still. How does one even go about this? Finding out what the needs of five partners are? It's going to take time.

I shake my head. It all feels overwhelming, and I don't understand how I can go from being perfectly fine to terrified in a matter of seconds. Urien takes my face in his hands. "Breathe, Kari. This is why we're going slow."

I lean my forehead against his chest and he slips his arm around my shoulders. "I'm sorry."

"Why?" Kent asks. "It's going to take getting used to."

I nod, and Urien releases me. "Are you hungry?"

Yes, and at the same time no. My stomach is all mixed up, and I don't think I can eat. "You guys eat," I say. "I'll be back."

I slip up the stairs and across the large balcony towards Verys's room. My mind is craving calm and quiet, and right now, laying beside him is the most peace that I'm going to find.

CHAPTER TWO

VERYS

Everything hurts.

I stare at the ceiling over my bed and evaluate the state of myself. I'm not dead, so that's promising, but every muscle feels like it was ripped apart and stitched back together again. I know there was magic that kept me alive, so there's every chance that that's true. My body is telling me I shouldn't move, but I'm restless.

Consciousness came suddenly, and I've been still ever since. But I have the urge to move in spite of the pain. To prove to myself that I'm not completely broken. I don't even know how long I've been laying here.

I remember enough of what happened to put together the pieces. The fae male that came after Kari and seeing his decision to kill rather than capture. There wasn't any question in my mind about what to do, and no time. If I were in that situation this second, I would make the same choice. Kari's life is worth more than mine. Always.

And after, I don't remember much. Magic and

pleasure and light and saying yes. I know that's what saved me, and why I'm lying here in a daze of pain. Sitting upright, I'm stiff and my limbs feel awkward. I must have been unconscious for at least a couple of days. Maybe more. Especially since no one is present. I have no doubt that they're checking in, but I prefer that. There's no need for an audience and I don't want anyone to see me struggle.

It takes me longer than I would ever admit to get myself up and across the room. To pour a drink of water and wash myself with the liquid in the pitcher. It's the smallest thing I can think of, and feeling clean feels good, even if I can't trust my body enough to go all the way to the bathing chamber. During the war I was lucky—never had an injury this bad. But being on my feet is reassuring. Energizing.

I hear her as soon as she enters the room, but I say nothing. The sound of her steps tells me she's trying to be quiet. Her hands stroke the small of my back before slowly stretching around so that she's embracing me. Kari's fingers stretch across my stomach, feeling as much of me as she can with her small hands. Her forehead presses into my spine, holding me tight. Kari is easy to read anyway, but her emotions are plain in the way she's holding me. More than she's able to say out loud.

More than I'm able to say too, though we both feel it. I place one of my hands over hers.

I don't know if it's the way she's touching me, or the fact that I can feel that she's very, very, naked behind me, but my body responds. I'm naked too, and the last thing I remember before waking up—aside from a few blurry images—is Kari riding me. Blinding light and pleasure that I've never experienced in my life until now.

"Does it hurt?" She asks.

"Yes." There's no point in lying. "But I can handle it."

"I'm sorry," Her voice breaks.

She feels guilty, and she absolutely shouldn't. I turn in her arms so I can hold against me and show her how aroused I am by her presence.

The tempo of her heart increases and the little gasp she makes as I press us together is precious. I like the way her cheeks tinge the light pink when she blushes, and the way she bites her lip. Her hair is wet, and the scent of her arousal is already strong. Floral and sweet. I can guess why, and I laugh internally. Someone had a busy morning. Too bad I missed it. "Why are you sorry? You didn't attack me."

"But it was because of me."

I stroke my hand down the side of her face before weaving my fingers into her hair and guiding her gaze to mine. I don't want her to look away. "It is a privilege to protect you, Kari, and I would do it again. Will do it again. I will do it as many times as it takes, because losing you..."

I watch the way her eyes brighten with tears as I speak, and I'm glad that I was never with anyone else. I can't imagine it. Don't ever want to imagine it. "Losing you is unthinkable to me."

She closes her eyes, and tears spill over. She tucks her head against my chest to hide them, and we stand frozen in this moment. I can feel her anxiety, how much she was scared for my life, and how it would have devastated her if I hadn't been as lucky. But she could live through it. I'm not sure I could. Not after everything.

But I also sense more. These tears are not solely for me. Nor should they be. Kari has been through more than most humans experience in a lifetime. And the changes are by no means small.

For a few minutes, we simply breathe together. It helps, staying still. Doesn't hurt nearly as much. And the steadiness brings ease back to her breath. "I didn't leave you alone," she says. "Last night was the first time."

I can't help but smile. "Do you think I'm going to be upset with you because you weren't glued to my side while I was unconscious?" I tip her face up so I can see her eyes again. "You're being too hard on yourself."

"You all didn't leave me alone for a second."

I laugh, even though it makes my body ache. "There are also five of us. And as much as I like and respect the other males in this house, I'm perfectly fine not being cuddled by them."

She opens her mouth like she's going to protest, and I silence whatever she would have said with a kiss. I've only kissed her once, when she asked me to. And only touched her when one or the other of us needed healing. This is just for me.

Her mouth is soft under mine, body going pliant and relaxed as I kiss her. Completely the opposite of mine. She just makes me harder. "Are you sure?" she asks, pulling away.

"After the way you saved my life, I think it's a little late to ask that."

Kari blushes. "That was different. We didn't have a choice. I want everything else to be…" she hesitates. Her fingers move a little on my back, just barely squeezing and letting go, and she takes a deep breath. "You've really never been touched?"

"Only once," I say. "Only by you."

"Can I?"

"Touch me?" I grin. "More than you already are?"

She nods, drawing her hands up to my shoulders,

and I shudder. A faint stirring of magic moves under my skin, at once strange and familiar. "Yes." I don't have the words to tell her how much I want her to touch me. Everywhere. My cock is trapped between us, hard as a rock, and there's no denying how aware of it we are.

"Will this help heal you?" Her fingers are brushing across my chest and the sound that comes from me is feral. "It might, but I could give a damn. I just want to feel you."

There's a fiery spark in her eye as she smiles, leans in, and grazes her teeth across my nipple. My breath goes short, and I find myself watching her, unable to look away. Reaching between us, she touches me. Barely. Chills roll across my skin and down my spine and I groan as she wraps her hand around me, barely able to close her fingers.

I know that nobody believed me when I said I was celibate—that they thought I used pleasure in private to stoke secret magic and hid it from the world. I let them think it, but I never did. There wasn't any part of me that wanted the magic of the Carnal Court until Kari. And still I could live without the magic as long as I am near her. But now…I want everything. She makes me want everything.

Kari looks up at me as she strokes my cock

slowly, and I feel good. So delicious that it makes my knees go weak, and I'm suddenly barely upright. I grip the stand behind me to keep from falling.

But Kari doesn't keep herself upright. She sinks gracefully to her knees and I curse when I see her tongue. *Feel* it.

I'm no stranger to sex. I've seen the rituals and the orgies and I've heard the talk of what a woman's mouth can do to a cock.

They were all fucking liars.

Kari's lips slip over me, and all I see is white. Pleasure and magic rush through me together, seeking out the wound in my side, knitting it together and making it more whole. Not complete, but better, and then the magic spreads to the rest of me, bringing my nerves to attention and infuses them with bright, silvery sensation. I've never felt my own magic like this—powerful and full. It's only ever been a whisper. This is a flood.

She sinks down onto me, and I can't even focus on what she's doing because all I can do is feel. Feel and grind my teeth together to keep from exploding.

Deeper and deeper she takes me and I'm overwhelmed by heat and wet and the fact this is *Kari*. She's choosing me, to give me pleasure. She still doesn't understand what that means here, how sacred and precious and—

Oh *Goddess,* what is she doing with her tongue? Everything feels like it's building, leading somewhere. I've seen this happen, now I know what it feels like, and it can't happen. "Wait," I say, pulling her away from my cock, "Wait, please."

She freezes.

"We can't."

Kari hesitates. "Are you all right?"

I scrub a hand across my face. "That was…incandescent. But I was about to finish."

She grins, reaching for me. "That's kind of the point."

"I know," I say, still having trouble forming words with this much pleasure ringing through my body. "But in your mouth."

Kari licks me, slowly. "I don't mind, Verys."

It's my turn to go still. "You would want that? Truly?"

She looks confused. "Do fae males not usually like that? Human ones do. Come to think of it, none of you have let me finish you like that." And then I realize. She doesn't know. She has no reason to, and she sees it on my face. "I missed something, didn't I?"

I nod, and pull her off the floor and into my arms. The wound barely gives a twinge. "And it's not a conversation we can have alone."

CHAPTER THREE

KARI

"Verys, put me down," I say, pushing on his chest. "You're not supposed to be walking, let alone carrying me, and I am *naked*."

He laughs softly, and I could learn to love that sound. It's so rare. "Every male in this house has seen you naked, and every one—including me now—has been inside you." His lips are at my ear, words making me blush hot. "Your scent tells me of your pleasure this morning, as does the fact that you're naked. You're going to have to get used to that. Being naked isn't uncommon in the Carnal Court."

We step out into the common room, and everyone's eyes flash to us. Immediately, the atmosphere changes. The fact that Verys is awake, holding me, and still fully erect with the remnants of my lips on his cock is a lot to process in a second.

Brae grins. "I see you're feeling better."

"Amazing what magic will do," Verys says as he sits on the couch with me in his lap, his cock pressing insistently and distractingly against my ass.

I clear my throat. "Was this really necessary?"

"Yes," he says. He looks at the rest of the men. "Kari gave me the gift of pleasure with her mouth, but I stopped her before—" he cuts himself off and starts again. "She doesn't know what she's offering, or what that would mean."

The fae in the room straighten slightly, and everyone looks mildly uncomfortable. Kent looks as confused as I am. I gesture to the room. "Can someone please tell me what is happening so I don't start thinking this is worse than it is? What is so bad about a blow job?"

Urien laughs and clears his throat. "You already know that females are the rarer sex. Relationships like this one," he opens his hands and gestures to the six of us, "are not uncommon, though usually the group has fewer members." There's a flicker of a smile. "We are mated, but not bound. There is a difference."

"Not unlike the way your cultures have unique marriage traditions, each of the courts have a mating ritual—though probably a better term would be 'sealing.' An act that binds two people who are mates together. Very unlike your mating traditions, it is not reversible." Brae says.

"Right," Aeric glances over at him. "So for obvious reasons, this is rare. Having a mate at all is considered a blessing. And still fewer seal that bond.

Some choose to exist in the state we currently occupy. Happy and committed, but not sealed."

"Why?" I ask, nerves bubbling up in my gut. "What does sealing do?"

"It binds you together in every way," Brae says, and I can feel Verys wrapping his arms around me slowly. Somehow he knows I need an anchor while I listen to Brae's words. "You can sense the other's feelings and magic. I'm told from those who are mated that there is no greater ecstasy, but if…something happens, then there is no greater pain."

I think about that for a second. They alluded to this before when we spoke about being mates. "I would be able to sense you. Like read your minds?"

"No," Aeric says. "None of us have experienced it first hand, but think of it as more emotional impressions. Echoes of what we would feel. Both the good and the bad."

I nod, trying to imagine what it would be like to have someone else's emotions in my head. Or wherever I would…feel them. "And why do fae choose not to seal that bond?"

Standing, Urien paces behind the couches, around the outer circle of the common area. "Some cannot bear to think of accepting something so permanent. Some do not want to risk the bond breaking. Like during the war."

Something clicks in my mind. "And in the Carnal Court that ritual is swallowing?" I'm trying to keep a straight face, because that's hilarious, but no one else seems to find it funny. Though I see a twitch of Kent's mouth out of the corner of my eye.

Verys presses his lips to my neck, and runs his fingers up and down my arms, making me aware of how close our bodies are again. "Yes. Though I have not partaken, here nothing is considered a greater gift than gifting selfless pleasure to someone. The magic that is created is very powerful. Consuming that magic, it's what seals the bond for mates. For others, it is simply pleasure."

"In all the courts, the sealing is in some way an act of selflessness and trust. That takes different forms," Urien adds.

The reverent way they speak about it makes me feel bad for wanting to laugh, and the clear longing in their tone makes my chest ache. But it's still a lot to take in. "And for us? How does that work?"

Brae shrugs. "Allwyn's magic always manages to surprise me and sometimes doesn't follow the rules that we expect it to. Though each of us would be bonded with *you*, I would guess that the magic becomes a net, and everyone would feel the echoes. The few instances I've seen of multiple bonded mates have been very in sync."

When Verys speaks, I jump. I was lost in imagining what that would be like. "If I had allowed you to do that, you would have bound yourself to me without your knowledge. I couldn't let that happen."

I turn, staring at him for a moment before pressing my mouth to his. It's good to understand. I was worried that he didn't want that, that it was something deeper that I had missed, and not his effort to protect me and my option to choose him.

And then Aeric speaks quietly. "Kari. It needs to be said that if you offered that, I would accept you in the same breath. But if that's not what you want, I am happy just living a life with you."

Quiet words of agreement are spoken from every male in the room, and the air goes still. But the reality of that sinks in. The sealing is unbreakable. Which means forever. Forever. They want me forever.

"You would be happy like that?" I don't address it to anyone in particular.

Aeric snorts. "Why would I want anyone else?"

"The goddess places things the way they need to be," Urien says. "I never envisioned myself sharing, and I never imagined being mated. Now I can't imagine anything else."

I look at Kent, and another thought hits me.

"Does sealing the bond stop me from having other partners?"

"No," Brae says immediately and firmly.

The pain in Kent's eyes is obvious, and the tension in the way he's keeping himself still as a statue. "I've said it before, Kari. Do not let me hold you back from something you want. I'm human. There's nothing I can do about that." He's on his feet and out the door into the garden before I can say anything else, and there's a flash of pain in my chest.

"Is there any way," I ask. "Anything that could bind Kent to me in the same way?"

Even without the ritual I can feel something settling and spreading between us. A connection that will never need words. "I do not know," Brae says, "But if this is the path we choose, I will do what I can to find a way."

I glance around at the rest of them, and find no opposition to that idea. They even nod. Good. "I'll be back."

Following Kent out to the garden, he's already disappeared. It takes me a few minutes of looking to find him in one of the little clearings, staring up at the scarlet sky. "Kent."

"It should bother me," he says, "sharing you. Or at least it feels like it should. But it doesn't. It doesn't even feel like sharing. More like…being a part of something bigger." He sighs, "I like that feeling, and I don't want to lose you. But I can't offer you what they can."

He turns, and the devastation on his face steals my breath. He steps closer to me, reaching out and barely brushing my hip. "I've been in love with you for a long time. And I want everything for you. I want you to be happy and loved and mated. And if I even get to be a small part of that, it's better than nothing at all. But please," he begs. "Know that if I could offer it to you, I would do it in a second."

I collapse the distance between us and let him kiss me. Kent's lips feel like a familiar homecoming, and I think they'll always feel like that. Like warmth and safety and comfort. Years of flirtation and longing come to life.

"You're going to be more than just a small part of it," I say. "Remember what you said to me? *If you thought that I'd leave you after all this, I don't know what else I can do to convince you.* The same goes for you. And they said they would try to find a way."

He quirks an eyebrow up. "Even Aeric?"

"Even him."

Kent kisses me again, this time more urgent, like he's relieved and full of joy and just wants to be close to me. I gasp under his lips. "Just remember that you being human doesn't ever make you less. Not to me. I'm human too."

"I know." He smooths his palms down my back and presses his forehead to mine. "I like it when you walk around naked. Reminds me of my fantasies when I would come into your shop."

"You fantasized about me?"

"Every. Goddamn. Day."

A giggle escapes me, and I press onto my toes to kiss him quickly. "Let's go back. This conversation isn't over yet."

No one has moved when we re-enter the common room, they were talking quietly, and now they're looking expectantly at me. "Why are you looking at me like that?" I sit down on the couch, grabbing a nearby blanket and cuddling underneath it. Being naked is sometimes a little too cold for my taste. But Kent doesn't let me sit alone, pulling me close and lending his heat against my back.

Brae spreads how hand, gesturing. "We're curious what you think. It's a lot to process, and a lot to think about. Especially for you."

"Why?" I'm not following.

"Because," Urien says. "There's a lot more risk. We'll be bonded with you, but you'll be bonded with four—hopefully five—of us. If something happens—"

"Bullshit." I cut him off. "You guys are taking the same risk. If I die, all five of you will be in just as much pain. If anything, it feels like you're taking the bigger leap. I'm human. Mortal. I'm going to die eventually."

No one says anything to that, but I feel Kent kiss the back of my head. That, at least, is something that we're in together.

I look around at each of them. They want me—*us*—for life, and the way makes me feel is brave and so much bigger than I can put into words. But I know one thing. "I love you," I say, and it's so true that it hurts. "All of you. And I don't care about the risk. I'm not going to let myself make decisions based on what might or might not happen."

Those words sit in the air, the continued threat to my life still hanging unspoken. "But I don't want to rush it either. You were right this morning, Brae. We have the time to figure it out, and it should be when we're ready, for each of us. And the rest of it… what's happening. I don't know what we're going to do about that."

Verys crosses to our couch, and sits next to me, pulling me over and into his arms. Kent pulls my legs into his lap, never breaking contact, never resisting the change. It still flattens me that it's so fluid and easy. That nobody's hackles are rising from possessiveness. I lay against Verys's chest, relaxing into his strength. It never left him fully, and now it's coming back in full force. His voice leaves no room for doubt. "I can say with certainty that not one of us will willingly let anything happen to you. And it's your choice. If you want to hide, we will shield you. If you choose to fight, we'll fight beside you. We are *yours*, Kari. Nothing else matters."

"Thank you," I say, pressing my lips to his skin.

That same feeling from earlier is here now, that settling of something. The web of tendrils between us that I can't name. But there's more, and I need to make a trip. "I need to go to the temple. The Goddess clearly wants something from me, and now that I'm here, and alive, I need to ask. Is there somewhere I can speak to her that's more…private?"

"Of course," Brae says. "It's a good idea. I'll accompany you, if you like."

I hesitate. "I think I need to be alone when I talk to her. But I'll admit that I don't want to go there by myself. After everything." Sitting up, I sigh. "I suppose I should put on some clothes."

Aeric laughs. "I would really prefer it if you didn't."

"You want me to walk all the way to the temple like this?" I ask, raising an eyebrow. "Everybody able to see me?"

"Hell yes," he says, not hiding the way he's looking me up and down. "Let everybody see how fucking delicious my mate is. If you want me to fuck you in the town square to show the Court how you moan, we can do that too."

I go bright red, and open my mouth to speak, but there's nothing. Finally, I manage to find my voice again. "Living here is going to take some getting used to."

They all dissolve into laughter, and soon I am too. God, how am I ever going to get used to this?

CHAPTER FOUR

KARI

How do you dress to meet a goddess? That's the question I'm asking myself as I'm standing in front of this closet that has way too many clothes. I'm not sure which clothes in here are from Kaya and which ones are from the house, but it reminds me of the costume closet at the ballet. Everything is beautiful, but some things I can't imagine ever having an occasion to wear.

But I suppose I actually have no idea. I'm not sure what my life is going to look like here in Allwyn. Will I be able to wear evening gowns regularly? I think again of what I wondered in the Crystal Court. What do fae do in their spare time? For fun?

The robe that I love which I discarded this morning is hanging back up, perfectly clean, as is that silky nightgown. I think I could get used to a world without laundry. Or cooking. Or any of the chores that this house takes care of. It's really not surprising that humans are so fascinated by Allwyn. This is every human's dream life.

In the end, does it even matter what I wear? I was

mostly out of it the last time I was in the temple, but I was naked. Everyone was naked. So I'm wondering if clothes are even permitted.

I opt for something simple enough, and close to what I'd wear on a casual day in New York. A simple red dress that I can pull over my head and falls to my knees. It gathers under my breasts and falls the rest of the way down. It actually reminds me of some of the costumes I used to dance in.

The way I look in the mirror is still jarring. I'm too thin—though the massive amount of food that the house keeps making will take care of that soon enough. But the skin and hair...I can't help but feel like a ghost. It's hard to meet my own eyes.

None of the guys seem to mind, but I don't feel like myself, and that's hard. I'm especially pale against the bright red of the dress, and I tear my gaze away from my reflection before I can get too caught up in my own thoughts about it.

Brae is already waiting for me at the bottom of the stairs, and he looks...normal. Like the fae version of jeans and a t-shirt. The short-sleeved shirt is tight to his body and showing me how *built* he is. I'd happily stare at him shirtless all day, but the way the fabric is stretching over his chest does funny things to my insides. Things that make me want to delay the trip to the temple. Down, girl. "You look very human," I say.

He smiles. "You assume that all fae dress like the humans imagine them? Fantastic things like leaves and *tunics*. Leggings?"

"I don't know," I say, laughing. "Just didn't think the fae wore t-shirts."

"What's to say that humans didn't get them from us?"

"Fair point."

"I think it's also fair point that both humans and fae make a lot of assumptions about each other, and that we're likely to be surprised quite a bit on both sides."

Brae takes my hand and guides me through the house towards the front door, which I've never had occasion to use. The entry to the house is beautiful, a small courtyard with pillars and a small bubbling fountain in the center. A painted galaxy swirls on the ceiling, sparkling with magic that makes it glitter like the actual night sky.

I guess calling it the front 'door' wouldn't be exactly accurate since there's no actual door. Just the entryway opening onto a stone path lined with colorful trees—birch and pine, or what looks like them. But like many of the other plants in our gardens, they are in colors and textures that you would never find in the human world.

A few feet from the marble of the entryway is the wall of wards. They glimmer in the air, geometrics and swirls opening and collapsing and reforming. As I look I feel like I see a different pattern every moment.

"How many wards did you guys put on this place?"

Brae's mouth tips up into a smirk. "All of them, I think."

"*All* of them?"

"We put up as many as we could think of, and Urien dug up a few more. There's everything from barring anyone but the six of us from entering without permission to keeping out external sound in case someone's sends an enchantment that's audible. We're taking no chances."

He steps through the wall of light and pulls me with him. It feels like a tingling breeze, and I can taste scraps of all of their magic. "Thank you."

"That's something that you never have to thank us for."

"And that I probably always will."

He squeezes my hand, but says nothing in response. I don't know that I'd be able to hear him anyway. I'm too busy looking around. This is the first time that I've left the house since I arrived, and it is a gorgeous assault on the senses. Everywhere I look there's something beautiful.

There are other walls and lanes that we pass, leading to other mansions hidden by trees. The air is rich with sweetness, and the bright light falls across the path we're walking with golden warmth. It's so much more than sex. Everything about this place caters to comfort and experience.

And for the first time since that day in the temple, I see other fae. Not many, but we pass a few others walking in the opposite direction. Beautiful and happy, and totally at peace. It feels too good to be true, especially since we know that something is hunting me.

"Should we be worried," I ask Brae. "That Ariana and whoever she sends after me will hurt others?"

He shakes his head. "For the moment, she seems to have an incredibly singular focus. But if that changes, we will inform the Rialoia. Urien being who he is gives both the access and the credibility we need if for whatever reason we need to move quickly."

"Good."

We walk down the avenue, which is nothing like the streets I saw in the Crystal Court. It's spacious and quiet, but slowly, I see signs of more population and life. We pass through an archway that's grown out of two trees tangled together, with variegated leaves falling in a perfect shower. My heart skips a beat as we pass underneath it, because it feels too simple, just walking with my hand in Brae's. It feels…normal. What I might do with a boyfriend, though we both know that this is far more than that.

"I don't think I'll ever get used to how beautiful it all is."

Brae stops and looks around, pulling me closer so that he can wrap his arm around my waist before we continue on. "You will, and you won't. It will become your every day, but there will still be things that take your breath away. But I don't think you know how badly we all want for you to have that—this just become your every day."

"I want that too."

The space in front of us is large and open, with trees here and there twisting from the ground in rich colors. Beneath the branches are pillows and blankets, with people entwined. Some of them are enjoying each other's company, and some are enjoying more than that. My eyes stop on a couple slowly making love, and it's so clear that they're in sync. Even breathing together.

They're not the only ones either. Just as many people are engaged in pleasure and sex as those that aren't, and there's something beautiful about the fact that it's just...happening in the open. No judgement or hesitation. No questions.

But it's still strange to see. "Is it rude to stare here?"

Brae steps behind me, just letting me rest against him. "No, it's not. If someone has chosen to be open and in public, they welcome your gaze."

"Okay."

He leans down and kisses my shoulder. "I'm torn between wanting what Aeric spoke of—to take you here where everyone can see—or to keep our pleasure where it is only us."

I can see benefits to both. "We have a lot to figure out, and there are things that I never imagined would be possible that I could try now."

"Really?" His voice is heavy with interest. "And what things would those be?"

I laugh, glad that he's behind me so that he won't see my blush. There are still some things I'm not ready to say out loud, and the thoughts and dreams I've had about all of them—and more than one of them—I'm not going to say out here in the open. I need the darkness and secrets of nighttime and kisses for those. "Not yet," I tell him. "Though you promised me when I woke up that you would continue what you started. You haven't yet."

"*Yet* is the key word there," he whispers. "But a promise is a promise, and if you think I've forgotten, you are *very* mistaken."

Shivers run across my skin. I want him. I wanted him before, but this is different. I'm healthy and healing and I want to be with him in a way where I can *participate*. Yes.

"You're getting distracted," he murmurs. "Let's go before I have to drag you back to the house."

Leaning my head back against his shoulder, I sigh. "This can wait."

"No it can't. It will drive you crazy. And we have a stop to make before we go to the temple."

"Where?"

He takes my hand again and pulls me to the left down a different street that's lined with blue stones and looks like it ends in a place with busier traffic. "The marketplace. It's not required, but I thought you might want to bring an offering."

"Like…a blood sacrifice?"

Brae's laugh echoes around us. "No, I'll show you."

The marketplace is like the one in the Crystal Court, and yet it's not. There's more people here than I've seen, and everyone seems to be enjoying themselves. But it's less chaotic than the Crystal market, even if it's just as crowded. Fae are moving at the pace that pleases them, and so the air is suffused with calm and happiness. Stores line a long avenue, the buildings in various shapes and colors. It disappears into the distance, and I realize I have no concept of size or distance in Allwyn. How big is the Carnal Court? How many fae live here?

I see a clothing store in a building that's jade green, carved with hundreds of flowers. A building that glimmers silver houses beautiful weapons of every kind. Fabric, magical items, flowers, even animals. Everything that you would find in the human world you could find here, and it's even more beautiful because it's fae, and likely magical. "Is there a sex toy store here?"

Brae grins. "Of course. I doubt we could call ourselves the Carnal Court without one. But I also know your other mates would be furious with me if I took you there without them."

"Fine," I say, rolling my eyes. "But I want to go there. And I want to take you all to one in the human world too sometime. Because I have a feeling that all of you would be like kids in a candy store."

"That is an excellent idea," he says. "We'll make it happen."

We stop in front of a building that reminds me, in a way, of the temple. The building is carved in flowing lines like a tent and is a deep crimson. At first glance it looks like it might be a flower shop, but as we walk closer, I realize that the only flowers that are present are roses. In every color imaginable. Combinations too. Right at the door there are emerald green ones trimmed in gold.

As soon as I step up and inside the air changes. The cheery noise from the crowd outside fades away and everything is still and sweet. It's cool and darker, but clear. Like taking a breath for the first time. "What is this place?"

"Where we'll find your offering."

"Roses?" I reach out to touch a flower that looks like flame. Red fading through orange and the palest yellow to the cool blue of heat.

"I suppose I didn't tell you that part of the story," Brae says softly. "When Cerys was consumed with her own fire, and remade Allwyn, roses appeared. Not only around her, but everywhere. Even in the darkest places in this world there were roses. Beauty and pain at once together. Roses are not native to the human world, and there's a reason that they're considered the most beautiful flower. The one that people give to represent love. That started here. Because to us, they represent the greatest love we've ever received."

It makes the flaming rose—so soft and innocent under my fingers—look very different. There's so much that humans owe Cerys too, and I don't think that anyone on that side has ever heard of her. Or if they have, they think she's a myth and nothing but a story.

The thought that the being who did that, who sacrificed everything for a world she had no obligation to save, has an interest in me is both humbling and terrifying. "Do you use them only for offerings?"

"No," Brae says. "Like in the human world, we use them for declarations and decorations. But they are never used lightly."

I nod, looking around at the sea of roses. I understand why this place feels full of reverence now. Why the temple in the Crystal Court was shaped as a rose. This is as close to a holy symbol as the fae have. And it speaks so many volumes without words.

"So if any of you buy me roses..." I trail off, not sure what I'm asking.

Brae turns me towards him. "Will it be a declaration of love deeper than we're capable of saying?" I nod. "Yes, Kari."

He kisses me, drawing me into his arms and wrapping me up until I don't know where we separate. He tastes like honey and sunshine. The magic sparking between us tingling on my lips and sparking outwards with little bits of light. And because I can—and because I want to—I kiss him back.

When he pulls back from me, still so close, we're both breathing harder. "I haven't had a chance to say it. I love you. You are my mate. And when I think that I may have lost you—that I may never have found you—I can't breathe."

I close my eyes against the sudden emotion threatening to spill over. There isn't a way to prepare for words like that, and I feel them so deeply. It could have been so easy for them to ignore the call of that magic. For me to die on that sidewalk in New York or in the dozen close calls we had, and I would not have the chance to live with these men. Even if I don't know why I was the one chosen for them.

It's me who kisses him this time, because I can't find words that satisfy what I want to convey. I throw everything into the kiss. Need and gratitude and longing and love so deep and real that I don't understand it. It will take me a lifetime to do so.

"I love you," I tell him when we break apart, and my chest aches with it. "And if you don't keep your promise to me soon I'll have no qualms about killing you in your sleep. I need you."

Brae's eyes go dark with lust at the same time that the sparkle with humor. "Yes, ma'am."

I turn back towards the impossible number of roses, but I don't let go of him, nor him of me. "What do I need to pick? Is there a number?"

"Whichever you're most drawn to. Nothing more complicated than that. As many as you like."

They're all incredibly beautiful, how do you choose? Brae walks with me down with the aisles of flowers, and I look. Petals that are sharp like blades and metallic gold. Electric green and blues and flowers that look like homegrown lightning. Crazy, and beautiful. But it's not till I reach the back of the room that I see it.

There's a bunch of flowers that tugs on me. *There.*

The petals are soft like velvet, and so dark that you could mistake them for black. But they're not black. Blue, purple, and green, all so dark you can't tell, swirled together so all you can see are the glimpses of color in the half-light. They're something so alien, so far a part from what I ever imagined a rose would be.

I feel that sense of *rightness* that I've grown used to looking for here. These are the flowers I need. There are seven of them, and it doesn't feel right to leave any of them behind. I gather them up, careful of the wicked-looking thorns.

"Happy?" Brae asks.

"Yes. Where do we pay?"

He shakes his head as we walk to the door. "You don't, for these. Offerings are not something that you make a profit from here. Anyone can take these to the temple if they choose."

Guiding me through the avenue towards the temple, I try to imagine a place in the human world where something like that could happen. It would be rare, if it could happen at all.

So much of fae culture is counter to what we were taught to believe. I don't know if that's because the only fae that humans can remember experiencing were those that tried to take advantage, or if we have a tendency to only see the bad. But all the same, even though I'm sure Allwyn has a dark side, the bright side is so much brighter than I ever hoped that it could be.

CHAPTER FIVE

KARI

The temple looks like I remember the last time Brae carried me inside it: a massive building of deep red stone formed like a tent blowing in the breeze. There are a few other colors mixed in here and there, but red is dominant. It speaks to lavish nights spent under the stars and near fires with a desert wind whispering in the dark.

We slow as we approach the entrance. "I'll wait as long as you need. Don't worry about the time. And if you need help connecting to magic, you can always ask." Brae kisses me lightly, and I smile at him.

I don't want to show him my nerves, even though I feel them. But it's not every day you go to try to speak to a goddess. One that clearly has a vested interest in your life. "I'll be back."

Entering the actual temple feels like deja vu. I'm glad that this time I'm entering on my own two feet. A priestess is there, completely naked except for gold at her wrists and neck. She's beautiful too, with dark brown skin and hair a deep red almost like mine used to be.

Her smile is serene. "You are Kari?"

I stop. "How did you know?"

"I was present for your healing. I am glad to see you alive."

"Me too," I say, looking away. It hadn't occurred to me that people might remember that. I don't want to be known by that attack or weakness. But I'm glad that she was there all the same.

"Why have you come, Kari?"

"I—" I have to take a breath and swallow. "I would like to speak to Cerys, if it's possible. She saved my life. She gave me four fae mates." I can't bring myself to say five out loud. "It seems that she wants something from me, and I felt like I needed to ask."

She nods. "Of course. You will need to remove your clothes."

I expected that. Placing the roses down briefly, I slip the dress over my head and put it on one of the waiting shelves. The only thing that's steeling my nerves is the fact that nudity is commonplace here, and people think nothing of it. The priestess doesn't even blink when I retrieve the roses and turn back to her. "Follow me."

She leads me down a familiar path through the carved stone, like through the layers of the tent. We pass rooms, some dark and some bright, all releasing the sounds of pleasure and ecstasy. When we reach the wide-open space that I remember, there's sex there too. Magic is thick in the air, even if it's not as many people as the last time I was present.

But we don't go into the alcove with the altar. Instead the priestess leads me through the path of writhing bodies and through the other side of the temple entirely. Here, we step into a small garden that's open to the sky. The high walls are the same red stone, and space is overflowing with roses at the edges. There's an open space of soft grass, lush and green, and there's an altar here too. This with a familiar statue of Cerys, though the scale is smaller than at the Crystal Court.

It's quiet here, with that peace that I've come to find so comforting. "I hope that you find what you seek," the priestess says, and bows slightly before she disappears.

I hope so too. But what do you do when you want to talk to a goddess? Just start talking? Think at her?

She seems to have answered me before…but this is…different.

I approach the statue slowly. The grass is soft under my feet, and I'm aware of the utter stillness around me. Placing the roses at the base of the statue, I sit in front of it, much like I did in the

Crystal Court with the Rialoia. Kneeling doesn't feel right, and since my gut is the only thing I have to go on, I follow it.

"I don't know why I'm here," I say softly. "I mean, I know why I'm here in the temple, but not *here*. In Allwyn. I know it can't be a coincidence that you gave me five fae mates—even if one of them tried to kill me. I just...

"I know I felt you when we were saving Verys. I know I did. And I have to believe there's a reason to all of this. I've had too much randomness in my life. Please tell me what you want. Why me?"

It has to have a meaning. It *has* to. The burst of magic that told me that Verys, Aeric, and Brae were my mates came *before* Ariana attacked me. Was that the reason why?

Despite what the wonderful men around me might say, I am not special. I have nothing to make this seem warranted. I'm just a girl from New York with a little bit of magic. Nothing more.

The garden stays still and peaceful around me, and even though nothing happens, its peace still sinks into me. I could sit here for a long time just absorbing that feeling that everything is right in the world. But I still don't have any answers.

Long enough passes, that I wonder if the silence *is* the answer. Perhaps I should go. Or maybe ask

Brae for the help that he offered. Maybe there's something that I'm doing wrong. Some step in a ritual that I missed. I close my eyes, resisting the urge to give into the endless spiral of questions that drag my mind down into panic and despair. "Please."

It's all I can think to say now. Everything I have.

Only stillness surrounds me.

Disappointment sits heavy on my shoulders. I shouldn't have hoped for this. Shouldn't have convinced myself that this is what I needed.

As I stand to leave, a cool breeze drifts against my skin, and my eyes catch on the roses I offered. They're breaking apart, petals floating on that air, and others from around the space joining them in a swirl of color and silk. It reminds me very much of the spell I cast that day, the roes swirling through each other in helixes.

"You summoned me?" The melodic whisper comes from behind me.

I jump, spinning to find the petals coalescing into a shape that looks almost human. Holy shit. I got an answer. I drop to my knees on the grass, bowing. I don't care what feels right now—if a literal goddess is standing in front of me, bowing is a good idea.

"That is...not necessary," the voice says again, words slow and deliberate. Her voice is rich. A sound like comfort—rain on the roof and the crackle of a winter fire. Wind through still trees. Whispered secrets. It sounds like memory. "I would much rather see your face."

When I look up, there's light. Light in the form of naked, glowing, woman. It's clear that it is Cerys, from the images that I've seen of her. Dark hair and beautiful features, not looking any older than I—though that is far from true. The rose petals shift inside her form, restlessly flowing through her power.

I have no idea what to say.

She looks at me, head tilted to the side, and she speaks slowly. "It has been...a very long time since I was summoned in a physical form. Forgive me. I am still remembering the reality of words."

Still speechless, I feel locked onto the ground. I can feel the grass between my fingers and toes, smell the floral richness in the air, and yet I cannot move.

Cerys looks at me again, and I see a spark of true interest and focus. "You are human."

"Yes, Goddess," I answer as if the words are pulled from me.

She steps closer, feet not touching the ground. When she places her hand on my cheek, there is nothing but warmth—no actual touch. Leaning down, she presses her lips to my forehead, and the garden disappears. I'm spinning through my life. My earliest memories and parents and the first time I went to dance class. School and boyfriends and training. The little moments with my friends. Birthdays on the beach and late nights in the city. The joy of getting accepted into the company and being promoted to a principal, and the night I fell. How hard I tried to recover, and how my dancing was never the same. The verdict that I would ruin my legs if I kept dancing, and the moment that my whole career disappeared. The potion shop and meeting Kent, longing for him. And finally now. The attacks and my mates and seeking her out.

When she releases me I'm gasping for breath. She knows my entire history, and it was shown to her in a second.

"You sought me out for answers."

"Yes, Goddess," I say again.

"Goddess…I suppose once." She wanders towards the walls with the roses and reaches out to touch them. "Such a beautiful thing." Golden light fills it, and it twists towards her hand reverently, now more alive than ever.

Nothing seems real. Can this actually be happening?

"You are not dreaming," she says calmly. "I have not stolen you away to a nightmare or worse.

Though what I have seen in your mind justifies the thought."

Finally, my voice makes a return. "Why did you choose me?"

The Goddess is still for a while, before she turns and looks at me. Those eyes filled with light are infinitely deep, and I have no ability to read what lies behind them. "Power is a strange thing. You only truly control it if it is entirely yours, and sometimes not even then."

I wait, because she's not finished. I know.

"My power is mine, and it is not mine. I use it. I sense it. But I gave it away."

Shaking my head, "I'm sorry, I don't understand."

"Do not be ashamed of that. It is not an easy thing. When I rebuilt this world I gave my power to it completely. And yet it is mine, and so I could not separate myself from it. I am Allwyn, and Allwyn is me. The power I relinquished is infused in this land, and it chooses for itself. Whether or not I am aware of it. Sometimes I am. Sometimes I am not. But we are still one."

Disappointment falls through me. She's saying that she doesn't know why this is happening to me.

"We choose things that are for the good of Allwyn and its people," she says. "Without fail. Some people call that fate, but things can change. Not everything is set in stone. If Ariana had not been stripped of her magic, she may not have entered your shop. Would you be bound with six males then? Perhaps not. But what might have been is now beyond reach, even for a Goddess. All that remains is what might be."

My jaw drops open. What? I didn't know that about Ariana, and she just said six. She confirmed it was six. That includes Kent. And the male who tried to kill me. But the gnawing question of *why* still swims in my chest. Why me? Out of everyone in the world? Why pick no one?

"I understand," she says. "You want more than I am able to give. I would show you my mind if it would not break yours. I am…fractured. I—We—Allwyn chooses. We do not always share thoughts. The connections not conscious, instead they are innate.

"But we have already chosen you. Woven you together with six others. For that reason alone, you are not no one. You must be here."

There. There's something. "Please," I ask. "Can you tell me why I'm here? Anything?"

She looks into the distance, the petals shifting inside her before she approaches me again. "Too many strands to see what might be changed. It is a knife-edge journey, falling one way or the other tangles all the strings. To know would shatter you, and betray the world's possibilities. But you, Kari, are where you are meant to be."

I look down at the ground, stunned by hearing the way she says my name. It's musical and enchanted, and I feel it resonate down to my bones.

"The magic you possess is special," she says softly, "but it is not enough."

This time when she touches me, the world erupts in fire. Bright white magic hurls itself outward and into me, and I'm burning with pure heat but not being destroyed. Magic is falling into my veins and burying itself in my bones and binding itself to who I am. It hurts, and it doesn't. It has me trapped and I've never felt more free. It's ecstasy and a shimmering waterfall of stars and glitter and fury. It's too much for one person to contain, and yet there's more still.

"You shall bear my power," the Goddess's voice whispers through my mind. "The power that is still only mine. You may wield it, or I may wield it, or we shall wield it together. You shall carry it until it is no longer needed. It will protect your mind from invasion. Shield your body from sickness, weakness, and child. Give you strength you never imagined."

It is hard to think against the storm of magic crashing down on me like a tsunami. But I'm not ready for this. I know she won't tell me the future, but I'm not sure that this is something I want. "Do I have a choice?" I ask, voice echoing in the magnificent place the magic has created.

"No," the Goddess says, though not unkindly. She's smiling at me as the light around her form fades, the petals inside swirling outwards throughout the garden again. "The strings cross and re-cross," she says. "Perhaps you and I will untangle it all. If you can survive."

She disappears then, and the final rush of magic shatters down onto me, and I lose myself in the brightness.

CHAPTER SIX

BRAE

It feels like an explosion of starlight in my chest, that burst of magic from the temple. Bigger than anything I've felt in a long time. It's Kari. It has to be, and I'm on my feet in a second. But this isn't dark magic. It's bright and soothing, and I know through that echo that connects us that she is safe.

I'm not going to break her trust by bursting in there. Not when she's already nervous and still learning to trust all of us and the fact that we love her. Not when she's still clearly nervous about having so many mates.

And she has a right to be. Being with five men would be daunting. I'm amazed we've done as well as we have so far, but it's only been a few days. There are bound to be some growing pains here and there as we figure things out. I know I've got questions. Is there going to be a schedule for sleeping in her bed? Will she ever want more than one of us at a time again? What will it be like if she seals the bond with one of us and decides she doesn't want any more than that?

It would hurt, but I would get over it. Because she's mine. That's never going to change, even if she belongs to the rest of them too. When we were talking about multiple mates this morning, I kept thinking there had to be some magic at play. We're fae males. I've seen jealousy become rampant in our relationships just as it is in human ones sometimes. But maybe the mating helps with that too. Eases our edges against each other so that we're not constantly at each other's throats.

Even if she chooses never to seal the bond with any of us, it doesn't change a thing for me. I meant what I said. I love her.

"Brae," a voice calls, and I look up. Lyassa is standing in the doorway to the temple. When I was still at the temple we participated in rituals together, and she is still incredibly beautiful. I used to dream of her often. But now she holds no appeal for me. The only person I can think about is Kari, and I know that that's the way it will always be. I meet Lyassa's worried eyes, and she beckons me. "Your mate needs you."

I do not hesitate. Stripping out of my clothes, I put them with Kari's. "The garden?" I ask.

"Yes."

I have the way there memorized. I have every inch of this place in my mind so well I could walk it in pitch blackness. I thought that this would be the place that I would spend much of my time in my life.

Now I'm not so sure.

I push through the curtain covering the entrance to the Goddess's Garden and take in the sight. Kari is laying in the grass unconscious, and peaceful. Rose petals are scattered across the grass and her body—including those she brought with her. But those are not the things that make my heart stutter. The first is that Kari is lit from within like a star. I have to squint my eyes just to look at her.

The kind of magic that is swimming under her skin is the same kind that exploded from her when we healed Verys. Pure and overwhelming. And the second is that she's whole. Her hair is that shimmering, rich red, her skin no longer the white of bone. I know before I reach her that when she opens her eyes they will be the green of sunshine through leaves.

I approach her slowly. The sight of her glimmering like an angel fallen from the sky is one that I want to preserve forever. Lyassa appears at the door, looking on, but I give her a nod. We're fine.

Sitting down beside her, I lift her into my arms. I don't know that there's another feeling I like more in the world than having her there. Which is why I choose to carry her when I can. I never imagined that I could feel so complete as when I have her close to me. I'll sit here as long as it takes for her to come awake, and to make sure she's all right.

But I know she is. I feel it in my gut.

Slowly, slowly, the light under her skin fades and she's just Kari. Kari as she once was before everything was stolen from her. She was beautiful on both counts, but I know it will make her heart easier to know that she looks like she imagines herself to be.

Lifting one of her hands, I press her palm to my lips. She moves just a little on my lap, and my cock responds. What I wouldn't do to spread her out in the grass and bury myself in her just like I promised her I would—but that's not what she needs at the moment.

"Kari," I say.

She opens her eyes and looks at me. "Brae." It's barely a whisper.

"I'm here." Her eyes fall closed again, like she's been utterly exhausted from what she experienced here. "Do you want me to take you home? Or stay at the temple."

"Home," she says softly.

She doesn't need to tell me twice. I don't even put her down to dress. Lyassa drapes our clothes over her and I stride out the door. Most if not all the members of the Carnal Court have seen me naked. It doesn't even make me pause. But I make sure that Kari is properly covered before we go. I'm not so possessive that I care about others seeing her naked, but I think she would be embarrassed if she had known she was carried bare in front of strangers.

Eventually I'm sure she'll lose the timidity, but her human sensibilities are still in the forefront of her mind.

It doesn't take us long to reach the mansion, and I don't stop until I reach her bedroom and lay her out on the bed. She stretches in her exhausted state, curling into the pillows that she loves so much. The temptation is too much, and I press my lips to her temple as she settles. I cover her with one of the soft blankets piled on her bed before I go searching for the others. There wasn't anyone in the common area when we passed, so I head to the line of rooms that belong to us. Aeric's is first. His room features deep burgundy walls and dark wood, along with some interesting accessories that I'm not sure Kari knows about yet—and the thought of her finding out about them arouses me more than I have time for at the moment.

"Let's go."

He looks up from polishing a sword. "You're back."

"Yes. We all need to be in her room. Now."

"Is she all right?"

I nod before striding down the row further. Verys's room is empty and so is Urien's. But Kent is writing out some kind of letter and nearly startles when I knock on the door. "She needs us."

He doesn't hesitate, jumping to his feet. For a moment it seemed like Kent was going to be a problem, but I'm impressed by the way he's folded himself into us. And by the same token the more I've gotten to know him the more I understand what Kari saw in him in the first place. He's loyal and kind, and once he got his head on straight hasn't shown the same possessiveness that he first displayed.

Aeric is leading Urien and Verys back from the other direction when I make it back to Kari's room, and they're all looking at me with wariness. After everything that's happened I would think the same.

"I don't know much," I say quietly as they gather around me. "I didn't go into the temple with her—she wanted to go alone. She was in there for a long time, and I did feel a blast of magic, but it was light. Pure. So I didn't interfere.

"Lyassa came out to retrieve me, and when I

found her she was like this, only glowing so brightly that I couldn't look straight at her. Her coloring is back, and she only roused long enough to confirm that she wanted to come home. Other than that, I have no idea what happened."

I watch that sink in, and then turn towards the door. And together we go see to our sleeping mate.

CHAPTER SEVEN

KARI

Magic feels like floating in the middle of a galaxy. Or having a galaxy shoved into your veins and behind your eyes. It's like seeing fireworks constantly. Like burning in a perfect way. Like sweetness and cream and honey and all good things. I've always known this—felt it with my little glimmer of magic.

But this is too much. This is a river where there should be a stream. I've been dropped off the Empire State Building and told I now have wings but I don't know how to use them.

I'm human.

I can't do this.

I'm not made to contain this much power. And without being told, I know that this is only a drop. Just skimming the surface of Cerys's true power, not even enough to cause a ripple. It's still enough that I can't comprehend it.

She said that it would break me, and she was right. This will destroy me. Consume me like it did her.

Will I smile when I go?

I can hear the murmur of male voices. I know those voices. They are *my* voices. Mine. I want them. But I can't seem to find my way out of this maze of magic. I'm not even sure where my body is. I feel different and I don't like it. Already too many things are different.

Reaching out with my mind, I try to find the boundaries of myself. Any little marker to show me the way back. I never thought that my own body would be a map that I could not read. I need the new code, the new flag, or the new key.

There—I can feel my fingers. Move them. Reach for something—anything. A hand takes mine, and suddenly there's magic on magic. Cool and silvery magic meets this bright and golden flame, and steam hisses when they meet. But the magic inside me likes it. It likes to play with others, and wants to learn. Wants to know more. So as that line of silver smooths over me the dazzling brightness retreats—folds in on itself until it's manageable and holds itself inside my borders. A solid spark of power at the core of me. So different from what I've recently held. This magic isn't going to steal anything from me. It's going to empower me and push me further.

I can't decide if that's what I want.

But I breathe sigh in relief all the same, because I

can open my eyes and not be blinded by it. Silver magic cradles me like a cocoon along with strong pale arms. Verys's long, lean body is pressed against my back, soothing me with that cooling touch.

There are other touches too. Hands in my hair and my feet are in someone's lap. "Hi," I say, opening my eyes to the concerned ones of my mates and lovers.

Brae reaches for my hand, and I let him take it, savoring the warm honey sweetness of the power that he adds, testing and probing to see if I'm whole. He must have carried me home. His voice is soft when he speaks. "Are you all right?"

I know already that that's a complicated question and that I do not have the answer. "I'm not hurt," I say.

"Will you tell us what happened?" Behind me, Verys's voice is rich and soothing, and there's no reason that they shouldn't know. And so I tell them. I start at the beginning and tell them everything. They're completely wrapped up in my words. Even Aeric, who's standing away from the rest of us against the wall. I can feel the intensity of his gaze from here.

As I'm speaking the words out loud, it doesn't seem real. How can this be possible? My logical brain tells me that Gods and Goddesses and power of this magnitude can't possibly exist. And yet magic exists. I've always had that inside me, and if that extraordinary thing can be real, so can this. I didn't doubt the story of Cerys when they told it to me, and I don't doubt it now. It just feels like so much. Too much.

Not one of them laughs or questions my sanity as I relay the goddess's cryptic words. Or her benediction with her power. "I don't understand," I say, when I reach the end, turning my face into the pillows. "I only have more questions. What am I supposed to do?"

No one says anything, and I can feel the fact that they're looking between each other. They don't have any more insight than I do. I can only grasp the fact that she gave me power. I don't know if it's to kill, to protect myself, or something else. But she thinks that I will need it, and that's fucking terrifying.

The bright center of that power shudders inside me, and I shiver.

"Nothing has changed," Aeric says. "We are going to protect you, and figure out what Ariana wants—why she wants you. It seems like that has to be the key, or at least a part of it."

"It is a great gift you've been given," Urien says, brushing his hand up and down my calf. "More protection than we alone can give you."

I sit up and out of Verys's arms. "I don't want to sound ungrateful, but this is *enough*." My voice breaks, and I hate that it does. Tears—of anger and panic—flood my eyes and the world blurs. It feels like everything that I was holding on to is slipping loose, and there wasn't much there to begin with. "I'm so happy that I found you," I say, voice catching in my throat. "But none of this was my choice, except for staying with you. This isn't why I went to see her. What if I hadn't gone? Would I still be this... conduit?" My breath is coming in gasps, and I'm dizzy, but I can't seem to stop the words spilling out of my mouth. "I never wanted a huge life filled with magic and adventure and battle. I can't do it. I *can't*. I can't. I can't."

"Kari," Kent's voice penetrates the fog and gets me to stop repeating the only words echoing in my mind. His hand curls around my neck and he's kneeling in front of me on the bed, face close. "Look at me."

I am looking at him. Clear gray eyes that bring me back to the ground, firm fingers giving me an anchor. I shake my head. "I can't do this."

"You can," he says. "I've seen you do *impossible* things. Including coming back to life when we thought we had lost you."

"I don't even know what I'm supposed to do," I

say. Every thought feels impossibly big. Infinite possibilities are in front of us, and we don't know which direction we're supposed to go. I don't survive in all those paths. The men around me probably don't all survive in all of them either. I can't. I need to go home.

Kent pulls me close, wrapping his other hand behind my back so that I'm pressed against him. "You didn't know what to do after the fall, but by the time I met you you had already come back from that and put yourself back together. You're doing it again. Aeric is right. Nothing has changed. Whether or not we had been given any hints, we would have—and still will—deal with whatever comes our way however we can. We're with you."

I know that he's right, I can feel it. But the itching of power under my skin is making my heart pound, and I can't stop envisioning the hundreds of millions of ways that things could go wrong. "I need to go home," I say. "Please, take me home."

He searches my face, knowing that when I say 'home,' that I don't mean here in this house with them. "Do you think that's going to change anything?"

"It might," I lie.

"Then we'll go," Verys says. "We'll take you to home. You can see your friends, visit your shop."

I'm grateful that he doesn't say what everyone is thinking, and that I won't actually be able to stay there, because it's not safe. I'm still being hunted whether I like it or not. But I need to get out of here. I need to feel something remotely normal and not be in this cycle of panic and dread that seems to be sweeping through me with the pulse of that new magic.

"Okay," I say. "Thank you."

Kent kisses me softly, but I don't want soft. Neither does the magic. It craves to burn and shine and *breathe*. I pull back and look at him, and then the rest of them. "I know that we're figuring things out, and that it will take time. But I don't want to think about anything right now, and I'm tired of the last time I was fucked being to save my life."

The air around me changes, charges, and Aeric raises an eyebrow. "Are you asking us to fuck you, Kari?"

"I'm not asking."

I'm still naked, and when he drags his eyes up and down my body, I shudder with the need that springs to life. Aeric's voice is low and full of sinful promise as he reaches and pulls me off the bed, away from Kent and against his body. "What kind of mate would I be if you had to tell me twice?"

Up close, Aeric's skin has marks that I've never

had the chance to notice. Almost like tattoos, swirling marks of barely darker green roll across his chest. I want to explore them with my mouth. I want to taste them—all of them. He doesn't give me the chance.

Aeric spins me against the wall, and I'm trapped against it, the cool stone making me shiver as he moves behind me. He is not gentle, and I do not want him to be. His foot knocks my legs apart, and the rustle of fabric before I feel his heat pressing against me. One large hand tangles in my hair, tilting my head back so I can just barely see him. He's hard and thick behind me, teasing me with just the edge of him.

Fuck, yes. Pleasure and magic and arousal rise up in me, and he's barely touched me. I'm wet—so wet it's like they didn't pin me down and pleasure me just hours ago. Will I ever have enough of the way they make me feel?

Please, Goddess, I hope not.

"Hands on the wall," he says, tightening his fingers. And that's all the warning I get. I brace my hands against the stone, and he plunges deep in one thrust. All my breath is gone, my eyes closed, mouth open. *Yes.*

Aeric's magic floods my senses. Mint and spices and pale green coolness. But unlike before, his magic catches the new magic churning inside me. It's not an invasion; it's a dance. And every movement is made of pleasure. He tilts my face back further so he can take my lips, capturing my breath along with everything else, and I moan into his mouth. This is what I want.

He releases my hair just long enough to catch my wrists where they're braced against the wall and hold them there. I'm pinned by his hands and his body as he plunges deeper, every stroke a beautiful friction that's making me shake. The way he's holding my arms still reminds me of that night with him in the Crystal Court, when he held my wrists much like this and pleasured me until I could not breathe for the sensation.

I'm almost there again.

Aeric is entirely pressed against my back, hard muscle and feverish heat sinking into me as he drives upwards, into me again and again, sending spears of magic up into my gut. They swirl and amplify and I'm hanging onto the edge, about to go over for the first time, unable to keep silent. Telling him yes. And more. And again. Harder.

He obliges. Teeth on my neck scrape my skin while he fucks harder, hands like bands of iron on my wrists. It feels good to be taken. I'm not sick. I'm not dying. This is what I want. Just us. My mates.

They belong to me just as much as I belong to them. The thought sends me over, shattering into screams and fractures of light.

I can taste his magic on my tongue, as if I'd swallowed a little piece of him. Spices like Christmas, rich and heady. He doesn't stop, rhythm never faltering and taking me higher. And higher still. Until he thrusts so deep I rise up on my toes, head falling back on his shoulder as he comes, pouring heat into me. Still, I can't move, trapped by his cock and his grip and his mouth on my neck.

He jerks inside me, wave after wave of heat flowing into me. And when he makes a sound so low, so feral against my skin, I nearly come again. Sagging against the wall, I lean into the fact that he's holding me. He slips out of me, and I feel the remnants of him spill down my thighs. "I love that you're mine," he says, turning to face him, and before I can say that I love that too, he consumes my lips.

I kiss him back, and put everything I feel into that kiss, because I love him. I love his protective streak and confidence, and the fact that he treats me like I'm not made of glass.

More heat appears at my side, and more hands on my skin, and I'm pulled into another kiss just as fierce. Urien. I gasp into his mouth, and when I pull back I see the rest of them looking at me. Hunger in their gazes. I shudder under the sheer force of it, and this new magic unfurls inside me, purring and reveling in the attention. It stretches like it's waking up fully, and I don't want that. Not now.

No. I tell the magic inside me. *No. This is for me. Please.*

Without warning, I find myself reaching out to the Goddess. I know she's real, and I know that she's listening. *I don't know what to do with this power. Not yet. But I want the magic that's between me and my mates. Something that's ours and no one else's.*

That fierce glow inside soothes and settles, and pulses with what I feel like might be an understanding so deep that it brings fresh tears to my eyes. And like a miracle, it fades into nothing but a faint shimmer. Dormant. There when I will need it but not pressing against the edges of my skin. It's like a sudden return to myself, and I nearly collapse in relief.

Wrapping my arms around Urien's neck, I pull him close and kiss him fiercely. Yes. More.

A second set of lips grazes my spine between my shoulder blades, and a third on my shoulder. Urien guides me back to my bed, and we collapse together onto it. He rolls me on top of him with ease, my back against his chest as he fits himself against me and thrusts in, his clear magic blowing through me like a cold wind of first frost and nightfall. He curls his arms around me, squeezing my breasts, teasing my nipples until they're so hard that they ache.

Urien thrusts into me with smooth, steady strokes. I'm already so sensitive that I'm half-way there, and the hands on my ankles startle me. Brae is over us, pulling my legs apart, watching Urien fuck me with dark eyes and a cock so hard that I want him too. Oh Goddess, is that a thing? I've never had more than one of them inside me at once. Never even thought of the possibility. But the thought now, the image that appears in my mind of being crushed between them with two hard cocks fucking me sends a rush of wetness to my pussy, and Urien slips deeper into me with a whispered curse.

Brae leans down and presses a slow kiss to my stomach. "You look so hot with him fucking you," he says, dragging a finger across my clit. "So wet. And I didn't get to taste you this morning."

Heat flings itself through my body, and I have to close my eyes. Urien does not miss a single stroke, driving up into me with enough force to make my gasp. Even when Brae's mouth meets my clit, tongue adding to the sensation and sunlight magic mixes with starlight magic beneath my skin he doesn't stop, arms locked around my waist.

Tiny strokes of Brae's tongue match Urien's pace

thrust for thrust, and pleasure flies up through me and out like a wave. I crash into a dizzying orgasm, ecstasy sharp and bright and fizzy. My voice echoes off the ceiling, and a Kent's mouth crashes down on mine, swallowing my cries. The expression on his face is one that I've never seen before, hungry and dark. "Tell them how much you like to be fucked," he says, voice low and rough.

"Yes," I say.

Kent shakes his head, and I can barely focus on his face, the next climax rising steadily like a wave. Magic has started to glow beneath my skin, swirling together, nighttime and daylight, contrasting and making every inch of me tingle and shiver. Now that I have nothing left to heal, the magic isn't consumed by a curse. Instead it bounces around inside, warming me up and increasing my capacity for perfect ecstasy.

The curl of Brae's tongue and the graze of his teeth make me tighten *everything*. Urien makes a low sound of desire, and fucks harder. Faster. I can't breathe, just on the edge of falling apart.

"Tell them," Kent says again. "You can do better than that."

"I can't," I breathe. "Too close."

He smirks. "Tell them, or I'll tell them not to make you come."

Brae smooths a hand up my stomach, magic easing my body as his mouth slows, and Urien kisses my neck, and he slows down too. Damn it, they're in it together. I close my eyes, trying to focus through the haze of pleasure enough to find my words. Where is the air? My voice? Anything besides the friction of cock hitting me at just the angle I need to explode.

Kent's hand cups the back of my neck. "Kari."

"I love being fucked," I say, forcing the words out, utterly breathless. And now that I've found the words they don't stop. "I like the way you feel inside me, stretching me open. Your tongue makes me wet, and I don't want you to ever stop." I can't breathe. "Please."

Brae laughs with his lips sealed firmly over my clit, sucking me deep and I arch away from Urien only to have Brae hold my hips in place so they both can resume their frantic pace. Kent is still kneeling beside me on the bed, eyes fierce, stroking his already hard cock. Aeric is with him now, and he drags his mouth across the skin of my breasts. Just adding fuel to the fire.

My orgasm is a supernova. All I see is white, and I'm lost to the fire of it all. Drowning in it. I told the truth. I don't want it to stop, and I'm telling them that. "Don't stop. Don't stop. *Don't stop.*" I'm begging them. Pleading.

Urien yells, thrusting deep and coming, wave after wave of heat and magic spilling through me and carrying me higher before I'm left limp and gasping under Brae and Aeric's mouths. Urien strokes my waist, kisses my neck, and doesn't move. His cock is still deep in me, filling me up and more.

"We're not ever going to stop. You're stuck with us, Kari." Kent says. Then, he grins down at me, eyes sliding down my body to take in the wonderland of pleasure. "And there's no bond to seal with me."

My eyes drop to his cock, and my mouth waters. I know what he's saying and I want to taste him again. The way Brae is sucking my clit in long deep pulls—even though I don't think my body can take anymore—has ripples of magic ebbing and flowing and my mind melted to nothing but desire and need. Aeric's lips tease my nipples, pulling them to taut peaks that ache from more of whatever he's offering.

I open my mouth, and Kent presses his cock between my lips, hissing with the pleasure. He's so hard, I already know that he's not going to last long, and neither am I. Brae is driving me towards another climax, and I don't think that I can. But if I've learned anything about these men and their magic, it's that I always underestimate their ability to tip my body over into light and freefall more times than I thought possible.

Kent's hand, still holding my head, guides my mouth deeper onto his shaft, and I love the feeling of his skin on my tongue. The light flavor of salt and mist that's uniquely him that I will probably crave forever. He groans, and I suck harder. That cocky smile is no longer on his face, instead his mouth falling open into moans that make me wetter under Brae's tongue.

"Fuck," he curses as I turn my head to take him more fully, swirling my tongue under the head of him, and his shaft jerks between my lips. Kent's hips thrust forward, pushing him deeper into me, and I don't stop licking. I use my tongue in time with way Brae is using his on me, and suddenly I'm on fire.

I cry out around Kent's cock, coming, mindless with sensation and powerless to do anything but let it roar through me. Rapture that intoxicates and overwhelms and shines. I hear the sound of Kent's yell, and I'm flooded with the taste of him. Goddess, I love the taste of him. I try to swallow it all, still lost in the throes of my own climax.

My heart is pounding when I can finally speak again. "You all are trying to kill me."

Brae smirks. "I think we've shown that we're

going out of our way to make sure that that *doesn't* happen."

"Well it's going to, if you keep giving me orgasms like that."

Urien slips out of me and pulls me down beside him on the bed. "That's a non-negotiable part of this, I'm afraid."

I try to scowl and fail completely. "I guess I'll just have to get used to it then."

"Yes," Verys says, from where he's standing by the bed. He's clearly aroused, desire clear in his eyes and the lines of his body, but he makes no move to touch me. "And before we forget, you should look in a mirror."

"Why? I'm probably a mess."

He smiles at me gently. "I think you'll want to see this." I narrow my eyes. What could he possibly want me to see? I don't really like looking in the mirror right now. "Trust me," he says, holding out his hand.

He helps me off the bed, and when the light in my closet glows warm, I gasp. *I'm me.*

I was right—I am a mess. The remnants of pleasure are on me, and I look thoroughly fucked, but I have color. My hair and skin and eyes are all back to what they were before. If anything they seem more vibrant. Even my lips, swollen from kissing, look normal. Who would have thought I missed the color of my lips that much? It's hard to admit how much I depend on my reflection, but having it back is everything. "She gave it back?"

"Maybe," Verys says. "Perhaps her power restored something in you."

"Thank you." I look over my shoulder and grin at him. "I'll trust you when you say you want me to look in the mirror now."

"Good." He says it sternly, but he's smiling too.

I notice that there are suitcases in the corner of the closet now. "Guess the house knows I'm going on a trip? I'll need to pack some things."

The glances that are shared don't slip by me. They're concerned, but not saying it. Brae nods. "Pack whatever you need. We'll make sure we're ready."

CHAPTER EIGHT

KENT

The letter is where I left it on the desk in my bedroom. It's a resignation letter. I figured we'd be going back to New York at some point, and I'm not going back to live there. My life is here now, wherever Kari is, that's where I'm going to be.

It's not like it's going to be a huge hardship to leave New York behind. I don't have family anymore, and though I enjoyed my job enough, it's not something that I lived for. It's good that I have the job I do, otherwise I'd be stepping back into the city with an NYPD manhunt on my hands. But the Magical Crimes department has always been a little more lenient, and dropping off the map has happened before. I can spin a story that makes enough sense that won't have the cops freaking out about a rogue fae roving through Manhattan. Now that Ariana is fixated on Kari, I'm sure that she's not a danger to the rest of the city.

I'm also very sure that the murder-spree of magic users I was tracking before all this started was because of her. The very crimes that I had warned Kari about the day she was attacked.

If I could go back alone and take care of things, I would. But she would never forgive me. She needs to go back, if only to see that she belongs here with us. It's going to be important for her, even if it's terrifying. I'm not used to having this kind of fear. But that changed the moment I thought she died. It's still in the forefront of my mind every goddamn day. I dream about it and wake up sweating. It's hard to process that that was only a little over a week ago.

I'm going to have nightmares about that day for the rest of my life.

For the second time today, Brae steps into the doorway of my room. This time he's accompanied by Aeric and Urien. Verys is still with Kari while she packs, and though none of us has said it out loud, none of us want her to be alone after her visit to the temple. Or ever, really. If we thought that she'd let us hover, all five of us would still be in that room with her.

"What's going on?" I gesture for them to enter.

Urien is the one who speaks first. "I wanted to ask for insight about what might happen in New York, and what you think Kari is looking for by going back?"

I shake my head, and sigh. "She's looking for

normalcy—any semblance of her old life. Probably seeking some kind of comfort that the rug hasn't been entirely ripped out from underneath her. But you know that. I'm not going to pretend to know her every thought. And if she thought you were trying to go around her instead of just talking to her she'd hand you your ass."

Aeric smirks, but Urien shakes his head. "You know that's not what we're doing, Kent."

"And I know that there's something you're not telling me." I've enjoyed getting to know these men over the past few days, but we're certainly not at the stage where we go to one another's rooms to hang out. They're here for a reason.

"Two more attempts on the wards," Aeric says. "Unsuccessful, obviously. And they were weak enough that I'm convinced they were just testing the boundaries."

I hold myself still intentionally, trying to temper my reaction. Fear and anger and the need to take action immediately spring up. But there's nothing to be done at the moment. Nothing has happened. But it could. "And you're worried that when we leave the grounds we'll be vulnerable."

"Not worried," Brae says. "We will be. She will be. And we'd be fools to think that Ariana is not watching."

Scrubbing my hand across my face, I stand and pace across the room to the bookshelf that's in here. It's filled with books on plenty of topics that I've been interested in over the years. The magic that fuels this place is truly remarkable. I turn just as Verys steps into the room.

I don't like puzzles that I'm unable to solve. It's one of the reasons I became a detective. That, and the memories that I quickly push aside. And the fact that we still don't know *why* Ariana is coming after Kari grates under my skin like dried sand. But in spite of the danger, this is necessary. "We can't make her stay here. She needs this. You know she does." I aim the comment towards the man who just entered, even though I'm itching to go make sure Kari is all right, he wouldn't have left her if she wasn't.

"She does," Verys agrees. "And I want to stay near her if I can. I know what it's like to suddenly be invaded by magic that's unfamiliar and unwanted."

I nod. He's made allusions to that before, though I don't know the full story. "So what precautions can we take?"

"Are we going to run into problems with human law enforcement if we're armed?"

There it is. "You shouldn't," I say. "As long as you don't carry the weapons in the open, and you don't use them on humans."

Brae nods. "We can do that. Obviously we have no interest in harming humans."

I let my hand fall on the letter I was writing. "I have some things to take care of while we're there. But they can be taken care of within a day."

"Do you think that she'll be ready to come back after a day?" Urien asks hopefully.

Shaking my head, I sigh. "No, I don't." I know why they're asking. It's that same sickening fear. Kari will never understand what it was like to watch her nearly die so many times. The thought of voluntarily escorting her into danger makes my stomach clench with nausea. But this won't be the last time that we have to do that, or the most severe. Even I could feel the magic rolling off her earlier.

"Is there a way to make a decoy?" I ask.

Aeric stretches his arms above his head and starts to pace back and forth, like he can't stand to stay still any longer. "That's what we were thinking. I don't know how bold Ariana will be in the human world, but given how we met I'm not taking any chances. We'll create a trail of portals that might buy us some time."

"Good," I say. "But you have to tell her. About that, and about the wards."

"I will," says Verys. No one argues with him. His

quiet steadiness will help with that news. "And I'll start working on the decoy trail," says Brae.

"Where can we go that's not here?" Aeric says. "If Ariana is trying to breach the defenses, she might seriously try. And maybe more importantly, where can we go that's just as secure but she won't know to look?"

I have no idea. My knowledge of Allwyn is limited—and most of it will be unhelpful in this situation. "It seems like we've created a pretty defensible place here, but other than that, I don't know."

"The Lunar Court." The words sound like they've been pulled from Verys by force, and Brae looks like he's seen a ghost. "Are you sure?"

"It's the last place anyone would think to look."

There's a tense silence in the air, one that's filled with years and layers of information that I'm not privy to.

Finally, Urien breaks it. "Will you be welcome?"

"That's unlikely, at least not by all. But hospitality will apply, if we really need it. They may not like it, but I can trust them not to harm Kari, and that's enough."

Brae shakes his head. "Your mother will be happy to see you at least."

Verys sighs deeply. "I'm sure she will. Hopefully we won't need to go there."

"Hopefully not," I say.

"Last resort," Brae adds.

There's nothing left to discuss, and everyone disperses as quickly as they gathered. Taking a deep breath and releasing it, I sit down on the bed. Some day, when all this is over, I hope that all this will become normal—that we can become the kind of cohesive family that I've heard the fae describe. But it's hard to worry about that when we have bigger problems. All I can do is believe that we'll be able to survive long enough to focus on the little ones.

CHAPTER NINE

KARI

Verys comes back into my room as I'm putting the last of the clothes I've selected into my suitcase. It feels a little weird to be packing clothes to go home, but that's the way it is. I'm looking forward to going back to New York, even if it's only for a few days. I want some things from my apartment and from the shop—keepsakes that I don't want to lose if I'm moving my life here permanently. Things like pictures of my family and my first pair of toe shoes. A few of my favorite decorative potion bottles. The pair of yoga pants that I've broken in so well they fit like a second skin and are so comfortable I used to live in them.

"Almost done?" he asks.

"Yeah," I say, pulling him closer. "And I wanted to ask if you're okay. Nothing…happened earlier. With you."

Verys smiles, and it makes my heart skip a beat. It's not the most common sight and every time he smiles like that—wide and open—it takes me by surprise. "You can say that we didn't have sex, Kari."

"I know." I make a face. "I'm not sure any of you realize how weird this is, or that unless you're drinking with your girlfriends at a bar, you don't just talk about your sex life."

"Not even with the people it involves?"

I sigh. "It's just going to take getting used to."

"You seem to be used to the sex and orgasms pretty well," he says, tucking a strand of hair behind my ear as I blush. "But I understand more than you think. In the same way, it's going to take me time to be open enough to participate with the others in that way. But don't ever think that means that I don't want you." He leans closer. "I need more private exploration before I will feel confident enough."

I like the sound of that. "You can explore me any time."

"I look forward to it." He hesitates, and I wait, because I can see that he's trying to find the right words. "There are things you need to know before we leave."

"Oh?" For the first time since earlier, that tiny spark of magic inside pulses, waking up. And it seems strange, but now...it feels more like me. More like *mine*.

"There have been attempts on the wards. Small ones. Testing it. The others think that she might follow us to the human world. We're going to be armed, and we're going to use decoys when we leave. Take every precaution. But it might not be enough."

I fight the dizzy feeling in my stomach. There's the residual taste of rotten orange and ash on my lips, along with the deep dread of disappointment. It's not like I didn't know. But somewhere in my brain I had myself convinced that I could go back and just open the shop and everything would be fine. Of course it's not. I can't ignore what's happening even if I want to. "Okay," I say. "But I still need to go. I need things from the human world, and I need to tell people that I'm alive."

I close my eyes as he presses a kiss to my temple. "We know, and we're with you. Forgive us if we're a little overzealous. Every one of us will be on edge."

I nod. They won't be the only ones.

It's only a few hours later that we're all standing in the common room of the house in front of a glowing portal. This is the way that I couldn't travel when I was ill—the vibrant pink rip in space is so bright that it makes me squint. The light is painting the walls and furniture, shimmering like moving reflections.

Kent has my small suitcase, and though they make light of it, they're all carrying magically-concealed weapons. Ones that are so sharp, I can't see there being any defense against them. They're taking this absolutely seriously. They might actually have to use the training they've been putting in. I didn't even consider that. This is *real*.

But I will say, one of my favorite parts of this is seeing them in human clothes. Jeans and t-shirts and henleys that make me want to rip those same clothes right off of them. They all look *damn* sexy, and Aeric and Urien have changed their skin color to look more human. They claim it's so that they'll draw less attention to themselves. But if they think that four sexy fae who look like *them* aren't going to draw stares they're absolutely fucking insane.

"Ready?" Aeric asks me.

I nod. They've explained what we're doing and how we're trying not to leave a magical trail that can be easily followed. Kent takes my hand as we step through the portal, and I don't really even have a chance to look around and see where they've brought us because another portal is opening up in front of us, a different color and a different place, and we just keep walking.

It's a really weird sensation, continuously walking and never moving anywhere. Going through the portal is a little dizzying. Magic pulls at the edges of me in buzzing waves, and I feel like I'm falling for a moment, though my feet never leave the ground. Every portal starts as a ball of light. Vivid blues and greens and golds. They expand and shift into jagged cuts through the world and as soon as they're open we step through.

Never once are they the same size, shape, or color. The only thing that makes them the same is the glowing, curling edges that throw off glimmers of magic like ripples in water. I pass through so many portals that I lose track of the time we spend walking through them. Kent's hand keeps me grounded, and I'm grateful for the anchor.

Every time we open one of the portals and step into a new place, we're laying a trace of magic for Ariana to follow if she's watching—and we all know that she is. The portal I step through this time feels like home, and it takes me a second to realize why. I'm not walking forward anymore. And suddenly familiar sounds and scents seep into my consciousness. New York.

We're in Central Park. A corner of it that isn't often crowded. The weight that's been sitting on my chest eases, and that new magic seems lighter. It's happier because I'm happier. I can *breathe.*

The sounds and the smells of the city—the trickle of voices from elsewhere in the park, and restless ambiance. Wind and cars and *noise.* There's something about Manhattan that eases my soul. I know there are plenty of people that would call me crazy.

That the idea of the hectic city being comforting is fundamentally opposed to their idea of what peace should be. But I love it just as much as I love Allwyn—more because I've loved it longer.

I expected it to be different, somehow. Like everything that's happened to me would somehow be reflected on the face of the city. But New York is New York, and it'll go on the same way no matter what happens. There's something a little comforting about that. From looking around, it looks like a normal, late-summer day here. It's warm enough, but I can feel that fall chill in the air.

Kent squeezes my hand and turns me to face him. "I need to go."

He's going to take care of things at his job and retrieve some things he wanted from his apartment. The rest of us have other plans. "Okay. Stay safe, please."

That lopsided grin I love so much flashes, and he's back to the cocky officer I fell in love with. "I'm always safe, Ma'am." He presses his lips to mine, and doesn't stop when I expect him to pull back. Instead he presses deeper, stealing the air from my lungs and leaving me breathless when he finally pulls away.

"If any of you want me to be able to function you're going to have to stop kissing me like that in public."

Kent only smirks. "See you soon."

He disappears down the path towards the edge of the park downtown. We need to go uptown, because our first stop is the store. It's not that far of a walk, and one I'm pretty familiar with. I used to get off the train at 59th and cut across the park on nice mornings. Because I'd much rather walk through Central Park than be trapped in the subway.

The guys form a loose circle around me, keeping an eye out for any potential danger, but I don't mind. All of this is perfect. I've missed this walk. I've missed seeing the yellow cabs and flower shops on the way up Amsterdam and rustle of Central Park's trees. *Normal.* It's what my mind has been craving. Even the first view of my little storefront makes something ease in my chest.

Urien puts his hand on the small of my back. "This is beautiful, Kari."

"Thank you." I step closer and look through the windows. It's exactly as I left it, except for the mail piling up behind the door and what looks like some notes that were slipped through the mail slot. But there's one catch. "I forgot that I don't have the keys."

"Not a problem," Aeric says, reaching out a hand. He covers the lock with his palm, and there's a subtle glow against the metal, and the lock clicks open. Right. Magic. I push the door open, forcing the pile of mail back, and we crowd inside. The scent is one of comfort and familiarity. Herbs and the remnants of the last magical fire that was lit. It smells like home.

But at the same time, it doesn't. Walking in here doesn't feel like I thought it would. I love that I'm here, and I love the memories that I had here, but I don't *miss* it. And it does make sense. I'm proud of what I built here, but anyone would have told you that I wasn't truly happy. I was trying to make a life only a few blocks away from the life that I really wanted. I was wasting away wishing for what didn't exist anymore.

In a way, I'm relieved. Even though it hasn't been long, my life in Allwyn doesn't feel like that. It feels full and perfect. And I'll happy to go back to it. It's good that I came here, because I know that now.

The guys file in behind me, and before I can even show them around they spread out, checking the corners for any hidden danger. Aeric slips into the back room for a few minutes, and nods when he returns. They all relax at once, agreeing that there's no immediate danger.

Brae slips into one of the comfortable chairs in the waiting area and stretches his legs out. "I can see waiting here for a potion or two."

I gather up the mail that's on the floor and carry

it over to the counter to sort through it. "I'm sure I could make you something if you wanted it," I say. "But I don't think if I unleashed brand new magic on a potion that I'd be able to tell you what kind of effects it would actually have."

There are bills and a ton of spam mail, and more than one hand-written note asking if I'm all right and where I am. That's nothing compared to the amount of voicemails on the store phone. And I hadn't even thought about emails, but I'm willing to bet if I check my business email that I'd be drowning in it.

Everything is intact, if a little dusty. I run my finger along a shelf of jars that hold the more common of my ingredients, and Urien appears by my side. "What are the things you wanted to retrieve?"

"There's a bit. But I don't know how I'll take anything with me."

"You don't have to. I'll send whatever you want to keep to the house."

I blink up at him. "You can do that?"

He leans in and presses a kiss to my forehead. "Of course. And the magic is small enough that it shouldn't be enough to track. We'll be fine."

"That's awesome!" I grab his hand and pull him into the back room. I'm sure there's nothing I have here that I can't get in Allwyn in abundance, but I have some things I want still. I have a shelf of bottles—both decorative and filled with rare spices and oils—that I've collected since I started the store. It's one of my favorite things here. In the afternoon the sun floods through the small window at the back of the store and illuminates the shelf that they're all sitting on. I can't wait to have these in my room in the mansion. "All of these."

I watch as Urien picks up a bottle, and it disappears in his hand as if it never existed, accompanied with a dark, shadowy burst of magic. "That's crazy."

"They'll be safe, I promise," he says.

I pick a few more things from my supplies, and some things around the rest of the shop. Some of my favorite books that I kept for the customers along with a few keepsakes. But when Urien and I have finished our circuit of the store, I feel good. I feel like the roots that I left here have been shifted, and that's a good thing.

"I have to take care of things here," I say. "Need to contact the landlord about breaking the lease and such, but I don't think I have anything more to do here at the moment."

Verys is standing near where he's left my suitcase. "Shall we go see your friends?"

Looking around the store, I feel more settled and

hopeful than I have in days. I'm calm and happy and I can't wait to take care of things and get back to my life with these amazing men. Closure. That's what this was. And I needed it.

"Yes," I say. "That sounds perfect."

CHAPTER TEN

KARI

I start walking outside of the store without thinking, my men flanking me. And it's not even until we're almost to Lincoln Center that I realize what a fucking idiot I am. I went on autopilot, and it's the same way I walked on *that day*. I turn the corner onto the street, and stop. I can't seem to make myself move any closer, and three of them know why.

"Muscle memory," I manage to spit out. "We should have come a different way."

Brae steps to my side. "We can go back," he says. "Go around."

We could. Or I could face it head-on. "No. No, I need to walk past that spot."

And I manage to get myself walking. But in my head I'm being pulled back to that day, and hearing her voice as she called to me from down the street. And then darkness and fire and pain. Ashes and oranges flood my senses, and pain ripples up my skin. She's killing me. I know she is. I thought we'd be safe and that she wouldn't find me.

"Kari." It's Verys' voice. But he wasn't there. Not until later. *"Kari."*

My vision clears, and I'm standing on a street with them, and Ariana is nowhere to be found. But I can still feel the echoes of that pain, and I'm there. *I'm there.* I can't breathe. More hands on me. And magic too. Magic that tangles with what's now mine and wakes it up. Another set of hands and more magic. "You're alive," Aeric says in my ear. "You're alive, Kari. She's not here."

"We've got you," Brae says.

This is a memory that I'm having. It's not real. She's not real. But it feels like it is. I can feel so vividly the way she made everything about who I am disappear, absorbing my power and my life. I remember hearing Kent's voice on the phone and knowing that it was going to be the last time. Realizing I never told him how I felt.

I can feel the way I was burning and see the way the color faded from the sky. But the sky is blue right now, and the air I'm hauling into my lungs is clean and not filled with smoke and pain. I lean into their embrace, letting them hold me up, and comfort me. She is not real.

She is not real.

I am not dying.

I open my eyes again into Verys's silver ones, and he smiles just a little. "There you are."

"I didn't expect that," I say.

"It's not uncommon," Brae says. "Or unnatural. I can't say that being in this place makes me feel good right now. But we're here, and she's not."

I take a deep breath. I'm here and she's not. All of us are here.

My heart starts to slow, and I inhale deeply, calming my breathing. I lean back against Aeric's body, letting him take my weight. He smooths his hands down my ribs, presses his lips just below my ear. His magic washes through me in one steady wave, washing away the lingering memories of bad magic. Aeric's magic isn't the magic I usually associate with being calm and steady. That goes to Brae. But right now it's a rock, grounding me.

"I'm okay," I say.

"It's fine if you're not," Aeric says roughly in my ear. "I'm not. I don't want to let you out of my sight or out of my arms for the next hundred years."

I cover the hands holding my waist with my own. "You have a deal," I say. "As soon as we get back to Allwyn." It's a promise that none of us believe that we can keep, but it feels good to say it.

"So this is where it happened?" Urien asks gently.

I nod. "Yeah."

"She's bold. To attack you somewhere so open."

"Indeed," Verys agrees. "She's not trying to disguise her efforts."

Even now, at a time when you wouldn't expect much foot traffic here, there are a few people walking down the street. More than one of them are looking at the way the three men have me pinned between them. Ariana either got luckier than she's ever been in her life, or there was a reason there was no one on the street. "It was a trap," I say. My voice is calm, but I am not. "There's no way that on this street with the Gala that night that I would have been alone. She planned it. How did she know where I'd be?"

Aeric pulls me more firmly against his body, and I see the fire in Verys's eyes as he presses his lips together. He's thought of it. They've all thought of it.

Urien is the one who speaks now. "It would be easy enough to divert humans with a simple barrier at either end of the street. It's likely that she followed you, picked the opportunity where she had to divert the least people, and struck."

I shake my head. I don't know why I didn't see it before. "Let's go. I don't want to stay here."

They don't hesitate, and we're moving around the corner into Hearst Plaza together. Immediately I feel better. To me, it's still one of the most beautiful places with the trees and strange sculpture pool. Whenever I come back to visit New York, this is one of the places I will go, I've already decided.

Funny how I'm already planning visits here like I'm from somewhere else. Goddess, this is absolutely insane. But this is the path I'm choosing, and I have to embrace it, even if I don't know the end or where the new magic inside me is leading.

I cross to the center of the Lincoln Center Plaza and perch myself up on the fountain in the middle of the tourists sitting there. It's late enough in the day that Emma and Odette will almost be done with rehearsal, and we decided to wait for them here, even though it's more open. I can't say that I don't feel jumpy after seeing that spot, but I walked *past* it, and that's the most important thing. No blonde woman in a black dress is coming to kill me.

Aeric didn't want to let go of me, but he did in order to fan out with the rest of the guys. It's better if I don't look like I'm surrounded by four men and drawing attention from tourists and locals. They also think that spreading out might help with the concentration of magic. But they're conspicuous even if they don't want to be. Even with 'normal' skin colors they're still tall, gorgeous men. They're going to get stared at. It's amusing to me that they think no one will notice.

I close my eyes and breathe, trying to center myself and letting the mist from the fountain cool my face.

All bets are off on what reaction I'm going to get from my friends. My phone was broken in the attack, and this is the fastest way to let them know that I'm alive. They're probably going to kill me. If the positions were reversed, I would be *furious*. The thing I'm counting on is that they know me well enough to at least let me explain.

The Goddess's magic—or my magic now—I'm honestly not sure what to call it, gets a little brighter. While I sit and wait, I reach down inside I touch it. Might as well. It's not a bonfire now. It's more like a match. Much easier to control, and the more it rests inside the less alien it feels. Though I'm not sure I'll ever get rid of the knowledge that this was *placed* in me. It's not really mine.

I've only ever used my little bit of magic, and that's just a thread. Even the small amount that I have cupped in my imaginary hands is more than I've ever had to work with. The way I sense it, it shimmers like glitter—one of those fireworks that's nothing but a shower of gold and silver sparks. It's diamonds in the sun. Undeniably gorgeous, dangerous, and alluring.

I move it around in my mind, drawing a few

shapes with it, and it bends to what I want it to do without hesitation. Far easier than I expect it to be. For some reason I thought I would have to push or fight with it, but I suppose that that doesn't make sense. It was a gift. I shouldn't need to fight with a gift.

Waving it back into a ball of light, I think about what I could do with this much magic. The Goddess said that I'd need it, so I'll need to practice with it. I haven't had a chance to ask the fae males to teach me more about it and how to use it. But maybe I can try something on my own.

Molding magic feels strange. I don't know if imagining it like holding coalesced light is the most effective technique, but for the moment it's working well enough. With that same ball that I just formed, I try a couple of more solid shapes first. A heart, a daisy, and then a star. Who knows if me imagining those shapes is doing anything at all but creating images in my head—but the guys will be able to tell.

Slowly, I push the magic away from me, towards Verys who's watching Broadway with sharp eyes.

I push the spear of magic out and out and out, not running out of power. It's exhilarating. I've never been able to do that! Softly, I touch Verys's shoulder. I can feel it and not feel it—like the echo of the feeling. He stiffens, whipping around, and his magic slices down on mine with a *crack!* that reverberates inside me. A yelp flies from me, startling a few of the tourists that are also sitting on the fountain, and the sound draws the eyes of every one of my mates.

I see Verys figure out what happened, and he's by my side in a second. "That was you?" His smile is relieved when I nod, and he pulls me in to kiss me in a way that's completely inappropriate in public. I love it, melting against his body. Verys has yet to kiss me like this, and if this is a sign of things to come, then I'll absolutely take it.

"That was very good," he says, and I'm gratified that he sounds just as breathless as I feel. "But keeping that magic contained right now is the best course. She already wants you for your own magic. Add Cerys's magic to that…"

Shit. I hadn't thought of that. "And I probably shouldn't startle you when you're already on the lookout for danger, huh?"

He chuckles. "That too, but I think I'm going to like teaching you to play with magic."

"You'll teach me?"

"Hell yes." His eyes are fierce. "We shouldn't be the only ones that get to have the fun. And I want you to be able to defend yourself."

That's perfect—I need to learn more about magic

and the echoes it leaves. I hadn't thought about the fact that maybe the Goddess's magic would only make me a more appealing target. But what little I know about Ariana, that is probably true. And I'm not about to let her catch me off-guard another time.

Verys kisses me. "I should go back to guard duty."

"But this is more fun," I say, pulling his lips to mine. Before I can consume him the way I'm really wanting to a voice echoes loudly across the plaza. "Kari?"

I look, and see Odette frozen in shock, and behind her is Emma. They're only still for a moment before they're running towards me, and Verys wisely gets out of the way. My friend—blonde ball of energy that she is—almost tackles me into the fountain. I hug her back, even though I can't breathe. Especially when Emma jumps on me too.

The tourists are looking at us like we're crazy, and maybe we are. But It feels so good to see them. Deep, aching emotion hits me all at once. I can't believe how much I missed them, and how many things that I need to tell them right now. Odette stands, and she doesn't keep her voice quiet. The expression on her face is no longer joyous. It's murderous. "Where the *fuck* have you been? We thought you were dead."

Emma takes her turn to hug me now without

tackling me. Quietly, but no less fierce. "She's right. We've been out of our minds. No word from you for two weeks and you show up looking like you went on a beach vacation, kissing one of the hottest men I've ever seen? What the hell, girl?"

I cringe. "You guys have every right to be pissed at me. But I'll explain everything, and you have to tell me shit too. But maybe not in front of the tourists." The last thing I need is for my story to end up on the internet. "Got some time to kill?"

"Absolutely," Odette says without hesitating. "Diner?"

"That'll work. But we'll have company." My men have gathered closer, and I point behind them.

Emma raises an eyebrow when she sees them. "Did you suddenly stumble upon a tree that grows beautiful men?"

"Just one part of the story."

She laughs. "Then let's go, because I have *got* to hear this. And I'm starving."

CHAPTER ELEVEN

KARI

Odette and Emma thread their arms through mine, and they don't let me go as we head to the nearby diner that we've always loved. It's the kind of diner that only people who live in Manhattan visit. Small, cramped, with a menu that serves everything from breakfast waffles to pastrami. We must look like some kind of celebrities, with four fae males walking around us like bodyguards. But it's nice to know that if anything is going to come at me, they'll see it first.

At the door to the diner, Brae stops me. "Take your time," he says. "We'll stay outside."

"Are you sure?"

He smiles softly and kisses my forehead. "You deserve some privacy with your friends. You know if you need us we'll hear you."

"Okay. Try not to make it look like this is a mob hangout."

"We'll do our best," Aeric says, smirking, and stealing a kiss. "No promises." I know he's doing it because my friends are watching, and their eyes are bugging out of their heads right now.

It's like they've never seen a flirty conversation or a kiss before, and I suppose that's fair. In the time we've known each other I've rarely dated. And even when I did date I didn't talk about my boyfriends or our sex lives. They're going to lose their shit when I tell them that I'm now involved with five men. At once. Hell, I'm still losing my shit about it.

"Let's go." I lead them into the diner and manage to snag the corner booth that we used to frequent when we were all in the corps together. Emma curls her legs up onto the bench seat beside her and stretches her foot against her hand. "Rough day," she says. "Feet are killing me."

"Trade me," Odette says. "I've been bored out of my mind."

Emma rolls her eyes. "Give it two more weeks, and you'll be fine, *Odette*."

I look at my friend. "*No.* You got it?"

Odette blushes. Ever since she was a kid she's wanted to play The Swan Queen in Swan Lake. It's not often that you get to play your namesake, and even though she's a principal now, it's early to be given a role like that. But her blush tells me that she did. "Holy fuck, congratulations!" I throw my arms around her as best I can in the booth. "That's amazing."

"Thanks," she says. She's being modest. Odette is an amazing dancer and watching her in Swan Lake is going to be magnificent. "But we have all the time in the world to talk about that. If you don't start telling me why you disappeared for two weeks and show up with body guards that look like they belong at New York Fashion Week, I'm going to scream at the top of my lungs."

"No you're not," I say, as the waitress approaches us.

Emma gives me a look. "She really will. I'll be right behind her."

We all order. The two of them omelettes and me waffles, and then Emma gestures. "Go on."

"It's a long story," I warn.

"Good thing I've got," Odette pretends to check a watch even though there's nothing on her wrist, "all fucking night."

"Okay."

It takes a while, and I start at the very beginning, from the time that I felt the strange burst of magic in the shop to putting on my dress and texting Odette to the attack. The frenzied journey across Allwyn and all the sex. I watch their eyes go wide as I describe what happen, and I have to look down at my plate of waffles and avoid their eyes during some of it. And they interrupt to tease me about Kent, because both of them know how hard I've been crushing on him for years.

I weave the story through the Crystal Court and through the final moments at the temple, and even through the attack at the mansion, the fact that I have *mates* and that I now have the magic of a Goddess living under my skin. The looks on their faces when I've finished are ones that I expected. They believe me, but even I know it's a story that pushes the boundaries of reality. I did skim over the exact details of some of the sex, because I don't even know how to describe what happened earlier today. But I think they get the gist.

"So they," Emma points to the windows and outside where Verys is standing in our line of sight, "are your mates?"

"Yeah," I say. "It's kind of hard to believe."

Odette shakes her head. "Damn, girl."

"I'm really sorry for disappearing," I say. "I wanted to see you guys get promoted."

"At first we thought that it was the gala," Emma says. "Figured that you got cold feet, didn't want anyone to talk about you, and decided you couldn't do it."

Odette takes a sip of her water. "But then you

weren't answering our texts. And after more than a day of not answering, I knew something was wrong. *Especially* when I went to the shop, and it was closed. And you didn't answer your door at your apartment. I even used the spare key."

"The police are bullshit, by the way," Emma says, tucking her feet up under her again. "We reported you missing, but since there was no sign of struggle at either place, they basically dismissed it. Said you'd probably gone to Vegas or something. That they'd look into it, but I don't think they did."

I open my mouth to say that I'm sorry again and Odette holds out a hand. "And don't apologize. You didn't exactly have a choice at the time."

"I know," I say, reaching out and grabbing that hand. "But I'm still sorry that you guys were worried. If I'd been able to get a message to you, I would have."

Emma pulls her dark hair back into a ponytail and grins. "Everything is forgiven, but you're going to have to give us more details about the sex."

My face turns bright red, and I can see the corner of Verys's mouth turn up into a smile outside. The bastard can hear us. I know he's not trying but being fae gives you advantages like that. "No fucking way."

"Lots of fucking, apparently," Odette retorts, and

they both laugh while I drop my face into my hands. "You guys are the worst."

"Actually I think we're the best," Emma says. "And does this mean we can come visit you? I want to spend some time in a house that does my laundry, thanks."

"Yes," I say. "Absolutely. Not until I know that you're not going to get attacked by just being around me, but I want to show you everything. It's so fucking beautiful. You have no idea."

While she's stealing some of the leftover syrup off my plate, Odette smirks at me. "If I'm visiting the Carnal Court am I going to be able to...you know... partake of the fun?"

Emma collapses into giggles and I cover my face. "Yeah, I don't see why not? They're all about it, as long as everyone is consenting."

"Fuck yes," Odette says, grinning. "Literally."

"I hate you both."

Emma leans over and rests her head on my shoulder. "You love us and we *missed* you. So are you going to introduce us to your boy toys?"

My eyes raise into my hairline. "I doubt they'll like being called that, but sure."

"They'll never know that we call them that."

I press my lips together to hide my smile. "At least one of them can hear you right now, so they'll definitely know." Emma's eyes go wide, and I smile wider. "Fae."

"That's going to take some getting used to," she says.

"You're telling me." I roll my eyes. "You guys want to introduce yourselves, Verys?"

He turns outside and winks before heading for the door. I swear that the entire diner goes silent when they walk in together. Everyone looks at them, because they stand out.

"I'm really jealous of you right now," Odette whispers.

"For once in my life I'm not even going to say that you shouldn't be."

She laughs as they approach, but Emma is the first one to stick her hand out to them. "I've heard some pretty good things about you guys."

"It's a pleasure to meet Kari's friends," Brae says, reaching out to take it. We do quick introductions, and I'm blushing because given what I just told them, I know they're imagining all the sex that we've had. But they barely blinked about the fact that these men are mine, and that I'm theirs. Probably because that's not even the strangest thing that I told them today.

"Did you have a good rehearsal?" Urien asks

them, and suddenly Emma is the one blushing. She nods and ducks her head.

"You know about our rehearsal?" Odette's voice is filled with shock.

Verys reaches across the table and takes my hand. "Kari mentioned that you were dancers." That simple act of taking my hand makes my stomach drop. I haven't...been in public with them. Not really. Because we're here in my world it feels more real, and more right.

Brae nods, and meets my eyes briefly. "When we arrived in New York and encountered Kari, we were on our way to a dance performance. And she's spoken about her own history. For obvious reasons, dancers hold a special place in our hearts."

I hadn't heard that, and Verys squeezes my hand gently.

"Okay, move," Emma says, standing up on the bench seat and literally climbing over me. She drops down and pushes me, forcing me towards Verys while I laugh. "We're not joined at the hip, Emma. I can sit away from them."

"Are you kidding?" She says, giving me one last shove. Verys helps her, scooping his arm around me and pulling me the rest of the way into his side. "I want to see this."

"We never saw her with any guys," Odette tells

them, whispering. "Now she has five. It's like the best form of people watching."

"I can hear you, Odette."

"So you're who we come to when we want the good stories?" Aeric asks. It's so strange to see him with a human skin color. I can't wait until we're alone and he's back to normal. My new magic can sense that something isn't...right with him and Urien. Like a nagging itch whenever I look at them.

"Yes," Emma says. "One hundred percent. We've got all the stories."

"There will be no stories!" I protest and glare at my friends. "None. Zip. It."

Verys kisses the back of my head in silent solidarity, but everyone else is laughing. "There will definitely be stories," Odette says. "Like the time she got locked out of the ballet dorm in nothing but her toe shoes."

"Odette—"

"We *definitely* want to hear about that," Urien says, cutting me off.

I sigh. "So this is how it's going to be? Everyone is just going to gang up on me?"

"Get used to it," Verys whispers. "We outnumber you."

"So unfair," I mutter.

Odette leans forward on her elbows. "How long will you be here?"

Before we left Allwyn, they tried to ask me how long I wanted to stay, and I didn't have an answer for them. It seemed so important to get back here, to feel something normal and real, and this has been perfect. I think I needed to see that everything was still here the way I left it.

"I'm not sure," I say. "I need to get some things from my apartment—"

In one movement, all of my mates swing their heads around and look out of the diner, and the feeling hits me a second later. It feels like an ache. Displaced nausea swelling in the direction that they're looking. All the magic I have strains away from it, trying to escape even the barest contact, and the waffles I just ate threaten to re-appear. But it's not her. It's not the feeling. I know that. But that sensation grows and sharpens and I can't breathe.

My fingers are gripping the edge of the table so hard that my fingers are white. Emma and Odette go silent immediately. "What's going on?"

"I'm not sure," Brae says.

My voice is raspy. "It's not her." All the eyes focus on me now, filled with appraisal and concern. "That's not her magic."

Aeric shakes his head and stands. "But it's not a coincidence either."

"What is that?" I ask. "That feeling."

"Dark magic," Urien says. "We'll go see what it is."

They all stand and I do too, and I see them getting ready to make me stay. "No. We'll be safer if we're all together. You guys come too," I say to Emma and Odette. I'm not leaving them here to suddenly be vulnerable as soon as we leave.

Aeric stares at me hard, and I think that he's going to push. But he clenches his jaw. "Stay back."

That, I can do. A wave of darkness spirals outward from that intangible place, and Verys pulls me out of the booth and towards the door quickly. I don't even have time to wonder where Urien got the stack of bills that he leaves on the table to cover our meal.

My friends are close beside me, quiet and tense. I don't know how to describe what's happening to them, but I'm grateful when they stay by my sides, watching to make sure I don't sway on my feet.

Walking isn't the easiest with that queasy feeling invading my mind. I've never had this kind of... awareness. Is this what it's like to be fae? To have things completely outside of you able to cripple you completely?

Urien trails behind us, but the other men lead the

way. Their hands are hovering at their sides. It's so easy to forget that they're armed, though I know full well that they're lethal even without weapons.

Walking up Broadway feels like wading through black sludge. My mind feels like a dirty window that I can't scrape clean, and it's only getting stronger. Sirens sound behind us, swelling in volume to the piercing wail caused by echoing off skyscrapers. One firetruck, and then two. They pass in a haze of shrill noise and screech around the corner just ahead. A corner that's very familiar to me, even through the fog of magic and nausea.

The reality hits me all at once, and I don't keep my promise. I start to run, passing Aeric and Brae, ignoring their calls for me to stop and pushing myself around the corner. The wave of dark magic is so strong, and the stench so powerful that I fall to my knees. The last pieces of my world seem to be falling around me.

My shop—the whole building—is entirely engulfed in flames.

CHAPTER TWELVE

KARI

"Kari," Verys's voice manages to penetrate as he pulls me to my feet. "We need to go."

I can't think. Can't breathe. The only thing I can do is watch as the place where I re-built my life burns. It's not a natural fire. I can feel the darkness pulsing from it as the fire consumes the building far faster than it should be able to.

Arms wrap around me. Odette, and then Emma. "Kari, I'm sorry."

I shake my head. My head won't process it. It's gone. Everything. I was just inside a few hours ago. We planned to go back, and everything seemed fine. But none of the decoys worked. We haven't even been in New York for six hours, and she's already here.

Shouting comes from the sidewalk, and I look over to see Kent sprinting towards me. He takes in the store, and then me, wrapped up in my friends. He's out of breath and pale, bent over from running. "I heard the call on the radio, and I knew…I thought you might..." Odette lets him pull me out of her arms and into his. "I thought you might still be inside."

I should feel more than this, I think. I shouldn't just feel blank—like nothing. But I can't tear my eyes away from the blaze, and all I feel is the push of whatever started that fire pushing against my new power. The magic is awake, and it wants to move. To strike back, and right now it's probably good that I don't know how.

"We need to go," Aeric says. "We can't just sit here. She knew that we weren't inside. This was to draw us out."

Kent's voice vibrates in his chest. He's still holding me. Should I be doing something? "Brae, can you track it?" He asks.

"I'm going to try."

"I'm going to get Emma and Odette home," Kent says, taking my face in my hands. "But we need to get you out of here."

"No," I say. Everything rushes back. Feelings and anger and desperation. "I can't leave. There are things I need—"

"From your apartment?" Kent asks. "We can't risk that. Not when she's destroyed this."

No. No, *please*. I can't lose that too. I feel the

panic rising in my chest and I hate it. I'm fucking *done* being helpless.

Urien steps up, hand on my arms. "I'll get your things, Kari. I'll make sure they're safe in Allwyn."

"My entire apartment?"

He gives me a grim smile. "Magic does have its perks."

Aeric holds out his hand to me and I take it. "We'll get Kari out. Urien, collect Kent once you're done and meet us at home."

I glance back at the burning building which is being sprayed down by both firetrucks and showing no signs of stopping—or any signs of spreading to the other buildings. "Home?"

"We need to fall back somewhere," Aeric says.

Emma's the one that pulls me into an embrace. "Go, Kari. Get out of here. Just don't disappear on us this time."

I hug her back, and I don't want to let go. Odette too. "I'll figure something out," I say. "I'll make them give me a phone or something so I can text you."

"You better," Odette says. "I need you alive for more details about the sex."

I roll my eyes, and she grins only the way Odette can at a time like this. Behind me, light shines. Verys has opened a portal, this one green and glimmering.

The abstract shapes spill little bits of magic like leaves onto the sidewalk. Home is on the other side, and with Verys's hand on the small of my back, we step through.

The last thing I see is the flames, and the roof of the building collapsing in a geyser of sparks. It hasn't even been a full day since I stood in this same entryway, and yet everything has changed. I'm so…so tired. We're standing just outside the wards, and I let myself get lost in the shifting patterns they create in the air. "Kari," Aeric says, turning to me, and his eyes go wide with shock.

Hands land on my body—unfamiliar hands. More than one set, and I'm being pulled away from Verys and Aeric. *We're outside the wards.* Magic explodes from me in one solid, bright flare. It fills the surrounding air with light, painting the walls of the mansion. It's like a nova, so bright I have to close my eyes, but the hands on my body fall away and I stumble towards my mates.

Verys catches me, and I look back to see a figure stunned on the ground. "Last resort," Aeric mutters, and Verys agrees. A blue portal opens beside us, and humid air blows through. "Where are we going?"

"We'll tell you when we get there," Aeric says. "Don't know who's listening here."

Through the gash of blue light there's an unfamiliar street in what looks like a sleepy town in the middle of the night. We step through. Then Verys is opening one that glows orange tinged with purple that leads us into a wind so strong it catches my clothes and I feel like I might be blown away.

I step through portal after portal, the sensation of being pulled from place to place making me dizzy. There's no way for me to track how many places we step through and away from. Until we stop. The sky is dark, though the moon shines bright and full above our heads. It takes me a moment to realize that is not *my* moon. Earth's moon.

The landscape around us is stark and pale, but beautiful in its simplicity. The three of us are standing on a hill, and laid out below us is a city that looks as bright and vibrant as any I've seen in Allwyn so far. But it's considerably smaller. Behind us a house rises on the hill, and an archway made from white stone. A path lined with columns leads to the entrance of the house, which is lit up with pale, silvery magic.

"We're in the Lunar Court," I say. "Aren't we?"

"Yes," Verys says.

I swallow. This is the place that hurt Verys. He loved this place even though it turned its back on him—was stripped away from him by Allwyn and his own family. I can't imagine what it must be like for him to stand here. Because of me. *For* me. He knew this was our destination when we first stepped through the portal. "How long has it been since you've been here?"

He laughs softly. "A very long time."

"Are you all right?"

"I'll be fine." His voice doesn't make me believe that. Not even for a second. "Let's go."

CHAPTER THIRTEEN

VERYS

I've spent a fair amount of time imagining what it would be like to see my childhood home again. I thought that I might be truly happy to see the place where I had the magic that I loved. I thought it might be difficult to face the place where I had known such pain.

The reality is somewhere in the middle. Memories swim to the surface, good and bad. The day I was thrown out of here by Darran and had no home left. The day I grew a tree in the garden with my magic, and I realized the world was full of possibilities. The moment I realized that my Lunar magic had left me, and that I chose to hide it for as long as I could because I didn't want to admit it.

But unexpectedly, I feel relief. I've been ignoring this world for far too long, and no matter what happens here I need to put it to rest. Kari's hand in mine steadies me as we step through the archway of the manor and the wards I know are placed there. They don't keep us out, but they alert my parents—my mother and Darran.

I glance over at Kari, curious what her reaction to this place will be. Seeing if she's all right. They were waiting for us, that fire meant to drive us home where they could ambush her. The attacker that she stunned with her magic didn't seem...right. But we should have been more aware from the beginning.

Kari's beautiful face is open and perfect and taking everything in. She doesn't realize, still, how much can be read on her face. I'm sure it's what part of what made her an amazing ballerina—that natural expressiveness. But as much as she's taking it in and seems curious, I know that she's hurting inside. Confused and tired and a hundred other things. I would be too if the world I'd built had just been destroyed. And I'd been attacked. Again.

As soon as we get this over with, I'm going to check on her.

The courtyard of this house is so achingly familiar, I have to blink to clear the memories from my eyes. White columns that support alcoves and recesses that disappear into the building. Windows that overlook the space. A fountain and garden. The courtyard was the life of this home when I was a child. I can't help but notice the absence of life now, barely anything growing in the dirt, and the tree that I grew long since removed.

"Verys?" The soft voice comes from across the

space. My chest aches. It's been a long time. My mother steps out of the shadows into the moonlight and she looks like she's seen a ghost. I suppose in a way I've become that to her. But it's only a second before she's crossing the space and drawing me close. "Hello, mother," I say softly.

She looks the same as she always has to me, absolutely beautiful. But as she pulls back from the hug and her face is illuminated by the moon, I feel Kari stiffen in shock. I should have warned her, but we didn't have time. It's not common for fae to have scars—at least not visible ones. And my mother is likely the first fae she's seen with any kind of physical imperfection.

The left side of my mother's face is covered with broken lines. They're beautiful in their own way, but also stark and jarring. They're meant to be a warning—a notice to all other inhabitants of Allwyn that she broke a vow that she made. I know that the scars—which extend down over her shoulder and the side of her body—cause her excruciating pain almost constantly. But she's never showed it, even for a second.

I sense his presence before I see him. "I didn't think my decision allowed for any exceptions." Darran steps into the light as well, and I feel Aeric go stiff behind me, ready for anything. Kari's hand goes still in mine, even though one arm is still wrapped around mother.

I meet his eyes without flinching. At least I can do that much. The pain I've buried long ago tries to surface, but I push it back down. Darran used to treat me like the son he thought I was. Even this eternity later, the reversal is jarring. "If I had another choice, I would make it."

"What could possibly bring you here without choice?"

"Sanctuary," I say.

My mother takes a step back, and her eyes are wide with concern. "Are you all right?"

"Clearly not," Darran mutters, "if he thinks he can seek sanctuary here."

Kari steps closer to me, placing her other hand on my arm, and I ball my free hand into a fist. The last thing I want is her exposed to Darran's poison, but truly, this is the last place that anyone would think to search for us, given my history and the fact that I've gone out of my way to sever all connection. I wish it made less sense. Familiar dread and rage rise up under my skin, and it takes everything to bite it back. "Unfortunately, it's a matter of life and death," I say. "My mate and I are requesting your hospitality."

My mother's eyes switch to Kari. "Your mate…" I

watch the news sink in. The last time she saw me I was being thrown out of here, and now I have a mate. It's like watching her realize all the life that I've lived without her. Pain fills her eyes, and it only adds to everything weighing on my chest. I never wanted to hurt her, and hopefully I'll get to talk to her about it.

But that moment of pain passes, and she straightens. "Yes," she says. "Absolutely."

"Siona," Darran hisses.

She turns a glare on him. "I don't care, Darran. I am not refusing hospitality to my son and his mate because you are uncomfortable. Goddess knows you've expressed your opinion on this subject more than enough times." Darran stares at her, and I think for a moment that he's going to argue. The muscles in his jaw are working, and I can feel restless magic slithering out from him. But he doesn't. He turns and stalks away, taking the cloud of tension with him. "Thank you," I tell my mother, and glance down beside me. "This is Kari."

My mother's smile lights up the courtyard like it's not the middle of the night and she wasn't woken by our abrupt entrance. She's always been a romantic above all things, and I know that when she was younger she dreamed of having a mate. This moment must be bittersweet for her. She steps forward and takes Kari's hands in hers. "It is lovely to meet you, Kari. I can't wait to know you better. But I imagine if you're arriving here, at this time, you must be tired."

"Thank you," Kari says. She seems subdued, and I'm not surprised. This would be overwhelming under good circumstances, and these aren't.

"This is Aeric," I say, stepping to the side so she can see him as well. "If it's all right, he'll spend the night, and the rest of our party will convene here in the morning to discuss a plan of action. But only Kari and I require hospitality."

"It's all right, Verys. However many people you need to stay can stay."

I shake my head. "We both know that's not true."

She can't quite meet my eyes when I say that, and there's an ache in my chest. I wish things were different for her, even if that means I would not be here. "Well, let's get you all settled, and we'll talk about it in the morning."

Taking Kari's hand in mine, we follow my mother through the house, and memories continue to pop out at me. I spent years here. But even so I don't realize where she's leading me until we arrive at my old rooms. They don't look the same. My mother puts her hand on my arm. "It is so good to see you."

I don't doubt the sincerity in her voice, and for the first time I wonder if I was wrong to stay away for all these years. I thought I was making things easier for her with Darran, but maybe I made it more difficult for her in a different way.

"Can we talk tomorrow?" she asks.

"Of course," I say. "I would love that."

She smiles, but I don't miss the sadness behind it. "Good. I'll see you in the morning then." She gestures to Aeric to follow her. But he doesn't. He steps to Kari and tilts her face to his. The way he kisses her makes me feel…jealous. Not that he's kissing her like that, but that I haven't. Even when she tried to offer me pleasure, it doesn't seem as intimate as that kiss.

I'm going to fix that.

"Good night," he tells her softly. "I'm going to go home to inform the others what happened and then return. I don't want the two of you alone." Aeric's quick glance at me and fleeting smirk tells me that he knows exactly what's about to happen, and he's giving me the opportunity to be with Kari without having to be on guard every moment. I'll make sure to thank him later.

Kari bites her bottom lip and smiles up at Aeric. "Night."

My mother's eyes are wide when Aeric pulls

away and turns to follow her, and I can't keep my own smile off my face. We'll explain it to her later, when Kari's had some time to rest and come to terms with everything. I know that she says she's fine, and perhaps the five of us are overprotective—we definitely are—but it doesn't change the fact that she almost died on us. And none of us ever want to feel that again. That attack just proved that the danger is still very real.

I pull Kari through the door to my old rooms, and I barely recognize them. They've been made into the consummate guest suite. Everything is delicately decorated in shades of silver and white, a gentle glow magically illuminating the space. I can only guess that turning it into a guest suite specifically was Darran's idea. Erase any sign of my presence and make sure if I ever return that I'll know that I'm considered less valuable than a guest.

But Kari is safe for the moment, and that's the most important thing.

There's a large pool, and it's steaming with heat. I spent my fair share of hours in it when I was younger, and I think she'll enjoy it now. Kari is standing in the middle of the room, staring into space. Softly, I let my hands drop onto her shoulders and down her arms. "Bath?"

"That sounds nice." She says, but her mind isn't in

it. If it were, she'd already be asking me questions. Turning her to face me, I lift her eyes to mine. "Are you all right?"

"I honestly don't know."

"That's all right. If I could take some of this from you, I would." Kari steps closer to me, and I wrap my arms around her. I can't describe the feeling... that rightness that seeps through my bones when I'm holding her. I never imagined that I could fit with another person, and now I cannot imagine my life without her in it. And I'm glad. Though I never would have admitted it to myself, I was floundering. I'm a warrior in a time of peace. I don't want war, but now I have something that I can protect.

I draw her towards the pool, hoping the lure of the hot water will coax her to open up. To relax and breathe. "I'm sorry about the store."

"It's fine," she says automatically, pulling off her dress.

"No," I say. "It's not. You worked hard to build that, and now it's gone. It's understandable to be shocked and upset. Especially with so many changes."

She sinks into the water, and the glow of it paints her body with light. I've spent so many years avoiding looking at people the way I'm looking at her now, trying to avoid any attraction or urge to connect. It still feels strange...but I keep my eyes on her. I let my gaze slide up her legs and the curve of her waist and further. Kari is the most beautiful woman I've ever seen. And I would think that whether or not she was my mate.

The sigh that comes from her as she dips herself down into the heat has my heart beating faster and my cock wakes up and pays attention. Suddenly my clothes seem like the least important thing that I could possibly have on my body. I throw them aside and follow her into the water as she dips lower, soaking her hair. "I mean it," she says softly. "Yes, I'm sad. And yes, I am *angry*. But one of the things I realized when we first visited this afternoon is that it didn't feel like home anymore. I got everything that truly meant something to me out. And so while I'm fucking furious at Ariana, I'm okay. I had insurance, and so did my landlord." She sighs. "And I don't even know what happened back at the house. That magic wasn't under my control but I'm glad that it happened. Seconds later we would have been inside the wards. But we're all right, and that's the most important thing."

I turn her to face me, because I'll know if she's telling the truth if I can see her expression. She is. I see the anger she's talking about, and the sadness. But I also see a determination that I haven't noticed before as well. This was the last straw for her, and now she will fight back. "Tomorrow," I say, "I'll start teaching you to control the power."

Kari's eyes spark with interest. "Why not tonight?"

"Tonight—if you'll let me—is for exploration."

"I already told you," she says, pushing me backwards so I'm sitting on one of the benches in the pool. She climbs onto my lap, and the feeling of her skin on mine, breasts pressed against my chest, is making me harder than I can ever remember being in my life. "You can explore me any time."

I slide my hands up her skin and pull her closer to me, until we're sealed together. No space left between us. "Any time is now."

CHAPTER FOURTEEN

KARI

I like Verys like this. His hands moving on my skin are bold, and his eyes are molten silver. There's no longer hesitance—only confidence. And he's still sweet. I know that if I hadn't told him I was fine, he would have curled up with me in bed and held me.

But I didn't lie. I'm okay. I'm livid and grieving for what I built, but I'm more angry than I am sad. Terrified that someone managed to put their hands on me again. And there's nothing I want more than to let Verys have his way with me. I want him to learn me in the same way that the other guys have had the chance to.

He's hard underneath me, and the way I'm straddling him I'm tempted to just sink down onto his cock. But I'm going to let him go at his pace, and right now his pace is touching me gently, sliding his thumbs over my nipples and watching with fascination as they harden. Cool, shimmering magic swims under his fingers, teasing me, and I close my eyes. "Yes," I tell him.

Verys strokes again, and arousal floods my system. I can barely stop myself from kissing him. Even so, my lips are drifting towards his. "I wouldn't know that you haven't really done this before."

A small smile appears on his face as he intentionally pinches my nipples between his fingers, power amplifying that pain and that pleasure. "It's strange," he says. "I tried to keep myself apart. Never participated, never let myself *want*. But believe me, Kari, I saw plenty. And I'm going to use every one of those memories to make you moan."

One of his hands drifts down between my legs, long fingers exploring with almost painful slowness. Even in the water, we can both feel how wet I've become, and Verys makes a low sound in his throat. He brushes across my clit and down to my entrance and back again. "You're going to kill me," I say, breathless, panting against his lips.

"I'm going to do a lot more than that. Everything has been crazed and hectic, and I'm going to take my time learning my mate."

I shiver in spite the heat of the water on my skin. There are goosebumps everywhere, magic tingling under the surface—both his and mine. My new magic is awake, alert, and ready to move. But it's not taking over. It's reacting against Verys's power and brightening inside. And maybe, this time, I'll be able to use it to tease him the same way that they do to me. Reaching between us, I grab his cock, and I just let the magic flow through my hand.

"Goddess," Verys says sharply.

"If that's anything like what it feels like when you give me your magic, this is more than fair payback."

He lifts me out of the water in one smooth motion and carries me to the bed. We tumble together onto it, his long body sprawling over mine. "You're a dangerous woman, Kari Taylor."

My snarky reply is lost when his lips hit my skin, sliding across my collarbone and to my shoulder, leaving silver sparkles and vibrations that echo through me and make me ache for more. Fuck. "I need you," I say.

"You have me," he says, mouth moving with purpose towards my breasts. I arch up under him as his lips cover me, sucking and causing a spike of pleasure that makes my eyes roll back. "You know that's not what I meant, Verys."

"I know," he's laughing against my skin. "And you'll get that. Eventually. But I have a long list of things on your body I want to get to know first."

He drags his lips to my other breast, grazing my nipple with his teeth, and I feel it in my clit. Magic spirals down through my skin and fuses to my bones and I don't know if I can be that patient. "You can explore later too," I say, a little desperate. "It doesn't have to be all at once."

Verys lifts himself long enough to press a silencing kiss to my lips. A kiss that drowns me with magic. More magic than I've felt from him. It's an onslaught of starlight that I'm caught in, a vortex of pure, shimmering enchantment. My own magic roars with gold fire in response, and I let myself fade into the pleasure of it all.

And while I'm lit afire with magic, Verys worships my body with deliberate reverence. His fingers leave streaks of silver on my skin that my magic burns bright after, chasing his lips and his touch down and across my body as he tastes each piece.

When he finally is between my legs, I'm already gasping with need, the echoes of arousal building on each other. But again, he explores me slowly—far too slowly. First with his fingers, seeking out every part of me, inside and out. His thumb strokes my clit firmly, toying with the direction and the pressure of his movements until I'm squirming. I manage to open my eyes long enough to see an expression of smug satisfaction before he slips a long finger inside my pussy and I have to close my eyes again.

He was right, he is making me moan. I can't

control it. My voice is being pulled from me, loud and desperate and begging for more.

"Hmm," he makes a curious sound. "I've heard them speak about a spot that makes females—especially human females—go crazy with pleasure. Now where did they say it was..."

Verys knows where it is. I can tell by his tone that he's teasing me, and that he knows more about what he's doing than he's letting on. But regardless he strokes his long finger inside me slowly, teasing me as he thrusts in and out. "Where could it be?" A cry escapes me as his finger brushes the rough patch of my G-spot, and he laughs softly. "Oh, there it is."

"You already knew," I moan.

"Yes, I did," he says, pressing a kiss between my breasts as he slips another finger inside me, fucking that spot with sudden and relentless rhythm. Pleasure shimmers just behind my eyes, and I'm so close that I'm shaking. "I'm going to come," I tell him.

"That's the idea, Kari." One more thrust of his fingers, and fire explodes outwards from that spot. The orgasm is deep, spinning through my core and crashing over my mind. I'm all shiny fire and perfection and my pussy bears down on his fingers, begging for more. And he gives it, sending me higher with two fingers and then three. I've flooded onto his hand, and I feel wrecked when he pulls away.

But he's not finished. His tongue is coated with pearly, silver magic as he touches my clit. A soft and subtle exploration, tasting what's left of my orgasm. "That day in the cave—the first time that Brae gave you pleasure—I could smell your arousal in the air. I've never been so tempted in my life. And I heard the others say that you tasted sweet. Now I know what they meant. You taste exquisite."

My entire body flushes with a wild mixture of embarrassment and desire. There's something wanton and sensual about him scenting my arousal, and the human sensibility that I shouldn't find it nearly as hot as I do. It shouldn't turn me on and make me wet, or the idea that he likes the taste of me. "Does being your mate make you find me delicious no matter what?"

Verys licks me, long and slow, and chuckles, the vibrations doing interesting things to my clit. "I've never heard of that. Magic rarely changes who you are. It amplifies it. No matter what, I would love the way you taste, and everything else about you." He seals his mouth over me and sucks deep, and my hands find his hair, pulling his face harder against me. I want more. That slow, steady movement is driving me mad in the best way. "And believe me when I say I'm going to taste you often," he murmurs against my skin, swirling his tongue around my clit and down to my entrance where he licks inside.

Sheer, pure, lust washes through me and I'm newly wet. His magic seeps in as he consumes me, showing me how thoroughly he's enjoying himself. No motion is frantic, instead each one is methodical, part of a sweeping memorization of my body. He's teasing me, noticing the way my hips thrust towards his mouth when he curls his tongue under my clit and the way my fingers tighten in his hair when he uses his teeth, and the way I squirm and get so much wetter when he sucks me deep and doesn't stop. All things I'm sure he'll use to his advantage in the future, and fuck I can't wait.

Verys draws my clit between his lips, sucking gently, rhythmically, as he teases me with his tongue. Magic matches every pull of his mouth, and sharp, fierce pleasure cuts through me. I'm past the point of no return, and I'm going to go over the edge. I'm going to come on his tongue, and I can't keep quiet. "Verys," I say, voice rough and unsteady. "Please."

His teeth graze me, causing my hips to rise to his mouth, and he drinks me in deeper. Presses harder. Verys's hands curve under my ass, lifting me to his mouth like he's feasting on me, and I'm blind with every sensation.

The climax takes me hard and fast, a rolling burst

of pleasure that sizzles along my nerves and makes me writhe under his mouth. The sound he makes as I flow onto his tongue makes me gasp. It's dark and feral and a very different Verys. I'm still in the throes of aftermath as he climbs up my body, and I realize that this is Verys *powerful*. For years he's kept himself separated from his magic, just existing with the little bit that Allwyn granted to him and nothing more. But now, his magic is growing because of me. With me. And it's overwhelming.

His eyes are shining with magic, glowing in a way none of the guys have before. Kind of like the way I glow when all of their magic is inside me. They're so bright I have to close my eyes as his mouth crashes onto mine. He steals my breath out of my lungs, and I love it.

"Have you explored enough?" I ask. I beg. "I need you."

Verys pulls back long enough to fit himself against me between my thighs. "I don't think it will ever be enough, Kari," he says. His voice is just as rough as mine, and he braces himself above me. Slowly, he sinks in to me. Verys is *long*. It feels like he just doesn't end as he presses his cock further and further into me, towards that deep place that not everyone can reach.

His eyes fall closed as he eases in, and I watch his

breath shorten to gasps. He was unconscious the last time he was inside me. For him, this is the first real time. Reaching out, I touch his face, drawing his eyes open and to mine. Those shining eyes are filled with awe and fire, and he kisses me again. Hard.

I'm full of him when he stops, and I can feel that he's not quite in all the way. There's too much of him, and I love it. Breaking the kiss, he presses his face into my neck. "Kari…you feel—" I squeeze down on his cock, and he goes silent, every muscle in his body tense. "Goddess."

There are so many things that I want to say, but none of them seem right at the moment. Instead, I wrap my legs around his hips, taking him just a fraction deeper. Sliding my hands down his ribs, I graze my nails up his back until I'm grasping his shoulders. I can see just enough of his body that I can glimpse where we're connected and notice the way his muscles tense as I rake my nails across his skin.

Verys's eyes are locked with mine, and he pulls back and thrusts deep, and everything erupts. His magic melds with mine, flowing together and flaring like molten metal. Bright, glowing, aflame. Light is glowing under our skin, shining on the walls.

He is so, so beautiful above me. All pale skin and shining light and awe. He's my mate, and for the first time I understand what that would mean. With all of them. I can feel the connection spun between us, more than just love or lust or desire. It's deeper than I can speak to, and I can only think of what it would be like when that bond is sealed. Will I be able to feel him like this? Sense more than just the echoes of what he's feeling?

I can feel his wonder and arousal and the reflection of his pleasure that's amplifying my own. And he thrusts again, melding more magic. We're like fallen stars, clinging together as we collapse out of the sky and into each other. There's nothing but bliss, nothing but him and the rhythm we're creating together.

Verys has already made my body sing, so I'm already falling into ecstasy as he presses deeper into me. I want this feeling with every one of my mates—being perfectly in sync and bathed in euphoria.

He's holding back. I know he is. He's trying to make it last and go slow so that he can bask in the experience. But I want more, and through that shimmering bond of magic I know that he does too.

"Verys," I say. "Take me. Don't hold back."

He does for a breath more, and then he falls into me. Lust and desperation and a hundred years of longing are unleashed all at once. He fucks me, hard. The magic is a storm inside me, whirling up and out in a riot of fiery pleasure. Every thrust sends me crashing over the edge again. I'm lost in him, dragging him closer as he moves inside me.

Higher and higher, I surrender to this connection, pulling Verys's lips to mine. He cries out into my mouth as he comes, plunging deep and holding himself there. Our magic blazes outwards in a wave together, and I seal my eyes against the brightness. Delicious heat spills into me, and my cries match Verys's. I'm clinging to him though, and he to me. He's pulsing inside me, magic and his own climax, and we're shaking together in the aftermath.

It takes a long time for me to surface again. But when I do we haven't moved. Verys is still buried inside me and our lips are still connected. His weight pins me to the bed, and I can feel the cadence of his breath—still fast—and the pounding of his heart. "And to think," I say, "all the members of the Carnal Court were missing out on that."

He laughs softly. "I'm sure my contribution would not have been missed."

"That's bullshit," I say immediately. "And you know it." But when he looks at me, I'm not sure that he does. "In case you didn't notice, I just had one of the best orgasms of my life?"

"Me too," he smirks.

I roll my eyes. "Smartass."

He kisses me, and I like the way he's grown more

comfortable and relaxed. "I very much enjoyed exploring you," he says softly. "And I can't wait to do it again."

"Any time," I say, laughing. "Within reason."

He shakes his head slowly, and presses his forehead to mine. "I've never felt magic like that. Even… before. When my magic was Lunar. It was never that powerful. And I barely know how to contain it all."

Reaching down to his ribs, I touch his side where he was wounded. "Did that—"

"It more than healed me," he says quickly. "There's enough magic in me now that I could take a hundred blasts like that one."

"Please don't. I don't think I could take seeing you fall like that again."

Slowly, Verys slips from me and rolls to the side. He pulls me against his body and covers us with a blanket. "It's the same way that we feel about you. Have any of us—" his hesitance is full of unspoken words. "Have any of us told you what it was like when we found you?"

Only scraps. I know what happened, the basics, but we've avoided talking about it for obvious reasons. "No."

He won't meet my eyes, but I can feel when he inhales to speak. I tuck my face into his chest, and his arms tighten around me, as if he can protect me from his memories. "You were gone. When Kent woke up he knew immediately, and he woke us seconds later. We still don't know how she managed to take you away without us waking. Assaulting Aeric was one thing, but there were three of us.

"As soon as we had the trail of magic, we ran. You were far enough that we almost didn't find you. But we ran into a wall of black magic. Dark, just like you felt at the fire. It's that same kind of feeling we had when you were attacked the first time. And it just made us run faster. But when we got there—" This time when his voice cuts off it's because of the emotion there.

"You were already gone. Your body was crawling with magic, and your color was missing. I thought you were dead, and you almost were. I've never felt anything like that before, Kari. I had just met you, and it was the most painful thing I'd ever experienced. The thought that you were gone, and I'd never had a chance to know you...I'll never forget that."

I press my lips to his skin, trying to soothe the pain in his voice. It's so close to the surface that it makes my chest ache.

Verys tilts my face up to his. "It was an easy choice to step in front of that magic, and I'd do it again. I will do it again, as many times as I have to."

"Don't say that."

"I will say it." His eyes are fervent. "And every one of your other mates would say the same."

I think about what the Goddess said to me. *It is a knife-edge journey, falling one way or the other tangles all the strings.* "I don't want any of you to die. Or sacrifice yourself for me."

A soft kiss on my lips. "I'd much rather live a life with you," he says. "I love you, more than I thought I could love anyone. But I will not hesitate."

I know better than to argue with him. I feel the same, and if I had the chance to save him—to save any of them—I know that I would take that chance. "I love you, too."

Verys pulls the blanket more firmly over the two of us. I have so many questions that I want to ask him about his life and his family here, but he's so warm, and after everything, I'm exhausted. I tell myself that I'm determined to stay awake, but as soon as I have the thought, I'm sinking down into rest.

CHAPTER FIFTEEN

VERYS

I wake up before Kari, when the bright is just beginning to lighten the sky. She's draped across my chest, and I love feeling her naked against me. I love feeling her breathe and the way her fingers curl against my skin even in sleep. The last thing I want to do is leave her and this bed. I'd much rather continue the exploration from last night. But this morning will be one of the few times I get to speak to my mother freely.

Darran sleeps later, and my mother does not. But I have a feeling the longer I'm here, the less inclined he'll be to let us have an open conversation.

Gently, I roll Kari over to her own pillow. She stirs but doesn't wake, and I can't help but smile. Her hair is wild, the vibrant red spread across the bed like a flame. Everything about the image is careless beauty. For as long as I live, I'll thank the Goddess and Allwyn for letting me be her mate. I'll never deserve it. And I can hardly believe that it's real.

I kiss her forehead before I leave, even though my cock is far more interested in staying. Last night was incredible. Part of me thinks that if I'd known that sex was like that, I would have never stayed away. And the rest of me knows that it would have never been like that with anyone else. The magic we created is more than us just being new to our respective power. It's about connection, and I could swear I felt what it might be like to have our mating bond sealed when I was inside her. Felt her longing for me as strongly as my own.

I feel strong today. The magic that crashed into me is still lingering. Like it suddenly realizes that it is welcome after all these years. I was perfectly content with the magic available to me, but this torrent makes it seem like the world is limitless. And it's all because of Kari sharing her body with me. I would not have chosen another way for this to happen. Because now this magic does not feel like poison and loss. It feels like vibrant love and acceptance. It feels like *mine* in a way that it never has before—Carnal magic has always felt alien to me. Like it didn't fit inside my skin. But now with Kari it feels the way I remember Lunar magic feeling. Like an extension of myself.

I feel whole, and I know that I'm still not as full of this magic as I could be. It sprung up between us so easily—I want to do it again. I wasn't lying last night. I could taste her forever. Bury myself in her forever. I'll never have enough of her sweetness and the look on her face when she's lost in the frenzy of her own climax.

If I keep reliving the things that we did together, I'm never going to leave this room. I find my clothes where I dropped them and dress quickly. Silently. If I'm right, my mother will be out on the hill, watching the bright arrive over the valley. She's always said she was lucky to have her favorite view in Allwyn right outside her back door. But I think that maybe that's not true, and she's made her peace with it.

The one time she went exploring, and reached beyond her limitations for something she wanted, she was punished. She knew she would be, and she did it anyway. That takes a unique kind of strength, and I've always admired her for chasing her happiness even though it's caused her near immeasurable pain.

She is where I thought she'd be, sitting on a bench on the edge of the hill, watching the bright rise over the city of the Lunar Court. It's chilly here—it nearly always is. There are few trees in the Lunar Court and the wind slices across the pale landscape. It can be sharp, and harsh. But this stark beauty is so much a part of my soul. As much as I enjoy my life in the Carnal Court now, after years, I miss it.

"You have embraced your magic," she says as I sit down beside her. "It's lovely."

Kari would likely be embarrassed to know that everyone in the house felt the magic that we created together, but there was so much of it I would not be surprised if people in the city felt traces.

"It is a recent change," I say. "Until I met Kari, I had no interest."

She doesn't look at me, but I see her hands tighten together. "I'm sorry that you have borne that pain."

The sky lightens, and I sigh, watching the city sparkle in the pale shine. "I have never blamed you. I hope you know that."

"I do. Though you have every reason to."

I shake my head. "I don't blame people for the actions of others."

"I'm sorry about Darran," she says quietly. "I had hoped that after all this time he would have softened in his feelings. That maybe it was just you showing up unexpectedly."

"I knew the risk when we came here," I say, reaching out and putting my hand on her shoulder. "The fact that he has separated himself from me so thoroughly is the one thing protecting us. No one would think to look for us here, though that didn't seem to matter in New York."

My mother smiles. "Tell me about your mate. She's human?"

"She is," I say, and I can't keep my own smile off my face. "And I am not her only mate."

"That explains that kiss last night," she says, raising an eyebrow.

I laugh. "Yes. It's been an adjustment for all of us."

"All of you?"

"Four fae males and a human male."

She freezes. "Five mates? That is…rare to say the least."

"Yes, and it's new enough that we're still figuring it all out." I give her a condensed version of how we met Kari and how we ended up here in the Lunar Court. "I am happy to see you," I say. "But I would not have come if we felt we had another choice. I don't want to cause any trouble for you with Darran."

"You are my son. You are welcome here any time you wish, regardless of his feelings. He has done enough."

I let my face drop into my hands. "You don't have to pretend with me. I know this will make your life more difficult. And if there were ever a way that you could visit us in the Carnal Court, then you would be more than welcome."

"I would like that," she says, voice wistful. We both know that it will never happen. Siona will never set foot in the Carnal Court again.

"How long?" I ask. "Do you think he will tolerate before we should leave?"

Her pale silver eyes—so much like mine—go hard. "You are under hospitality. Stay as long as you like."

"We will stay as long as our welcome does not cause you harm," I say. Darran hates me, and the longer I stay in his home the more that hatred will bleed over into his relationship with my mother. He does not harm her, and they have found a kind of peace after all these years, but it is not the life my mother wished for herself.

She smiles. "Your mate is awake."

I turn and find Kari watching us from the house, and I wave her out. I want her to meet Siona in a less hostile environment. Her eyes are still dazed with barely-shaken sleep, and I take the opportunity to pull her onto my lap—she doesn't resist. The way she fits against me is so tempting that I want to steal her away back to that bedroom and spend the day ignoring the rest of the world. I settle for a kiss that makes her blush.

"Morning," she says.

"Good morning. How did you sleep?"

Pink tinges her cheeks again. "It was wonderful. Thank you," she directs the words at my mother. "You have a very comfortable home."

"You're quite welcome, Kari," she says. "I'm glad that we can be a place of safety for you."

"I appreciate it," Kari says quietly.

"Hopefully we will know more today. Once the others arrive."

Kari nods firmly. "Good. I could use some answers."

"How long until the rest of your mates arrive?" My mother stands gracefully. "You should eat something while you wait. And perhaps I can get to know you better."

"I would love that," Kari says, standing.

My mother loops her arms through Kari's and pulls her into the house. I don't move to follow immediately, instead taking in the view that I've missed. Plains of pure white dust marred only by the walls of the city. Rolling hills in the distance with ruins of pale stone and the few trees casting long shadows across the land. I love that I can breathe here. I've always loved the wide open spaces of the Lunar Court. The Carnal Court can feel so close and crowded. But with Kari, it feels less oppressive.

And perhaps, after all this time, some of the damage that was done can heal.

Standing to follow Kari and my mother into the manor, I see Darran watching me from an upper window, face locked in anger. I very much hope the others have insight or answers. Because no matter what Siona insists, our welcome here will not remain solid for long.

CHAPTER SIXTEEN

KARI

Verys's mother is lovely. Her scars took me by surprise last night. I've never seen a fae with scars. And they're not faded either. They're red and angry, like whatever drew the intricate patterns on her face happened just yesterday. But I can tell that they're not fresh. She moves with them as if they're a part of her, not wincing or being careful the way you would if you had just been injured. But I can't imagine what would cause a scar like that, and one that doesn't seem to heal.

As we ate, she asked me about my past, and how I'm recovering. I'm not surprised that Verys told her a little about how we met, and what happened. Since it's why we're here. And it feels nice to talk honestly with someone about it. I'm recovering, but I keep getting knocked back. I'm angrier than I've ever felt in my life and I have no outlet for it. And of course I'm sad.

But if there's one thing that talking with Siona makes me realize, it's that I'm ready to fight back. I'm not just going to keep running and hiding. We have to make some kind of move, even if I'm not sure what that is yet.

"I want you to know that you are welcome here," Siona says. "No matter what anyone else says."

"Thank you."

She smiles warmly. "I have an appointment in the city, but I look forward to talking again soon."

Verys appears by my side as she leaves. "Your mother is wonderful."

"Yes, she is."

Nervousness wells in my stomach. "I was going to ask last night—"

"About the scars? I figured as much. It's not something you see often."

"What happened?"

Verys sighs and sits down at the table across from me. "Do you remember when I told you that Brae and I are half-brothers?"

I do, and I nod, though I've rarely seen any similarities between them.

"The parts of Allwyn you have seen are very open. Not all places are like the Carnal Court. Not all relationships are open, and if you take vows they are a serious matter. If you break them, there are consequences."

He said something about that when we were

traveling. *My mother broke her vows to her husband.* "What kind of vow?"

"Both Darran and Siona are from powerful families here in the Lunar Court. Their marriage was an alliance for power. Darran loved her, I think, but my mother married him because she felt it was the right thing to do at the time. There was political pressure, and they both agreed. Marriages in Allwyn can take different forms, and not all of them have vows. But because of the reason for the marriage in the first place vows were required, and vows in Allwyn are not like vows in the human world. When you make a vow here, you bind a piece of yourself to it."

"What happened?"

Verys smiles a little sadly. "She fell in love. Deeply. With someone else. My father. Brae's father. And she broke her vow to be with him. She knew that there would be scars, and she knew that she would be in pain for the rest of her life, but she did it anyway, because she loved him."

Pain every day. Now that I know what it's like to live in excruciating pain, I would never wish that on anyone. To know the consequences and do it anyway—that's a special kind of love. The kind I feel for Verys and the others.

"For obvious reasons, she wasn't able to hide what happened. Darran could have appealed to the

Court and to Allwyn to have her punished and stripped of her vow—which would have killed her—but he didn't. He forgave her, and let her see her lover because he knew it made Siona happy, and he loved her. Until it was discovered that his only son was not his, but a son of the Carnal Court."

"Verys…" I say. That's him.

"I was their only child, and the fact that not even that belonged to him was one betrayal too far. He made Siona swear new vows to him that bound her to the Lunar Court, and to him more tightly. If she wants to leave, he must grant her permission, otherwise she will die. Her life is very limited now, but even she is not foolish enough to break a second vow. That kind of magic takes a toll on you, and she would not survive it."

My heart aches for her and the pain she lives with. Not only is she trapped here, she's separated from both her lover and her son. I've already made the connection that it was Darran that kicked Verys out of the Lunar Court. "I'm sorry."

"It is what it is," Verys says, though his casual tone doesn't match his expression. "This all happened a long time ago."

"That doesn't make it easier."

"I suppose not."

We hang in silence for a moment.

"If I seal the mating bond with any of you, is that a vow?"

Verys shakes his head. "Sealing a bond that Allwyn wove between two people, and voluntarily taking a vow are different. You cannot choose a mate. But you can choose not to make a vow."

"Unless you're forced," I say quietly.

"Siona has found her own kind of happiness," Verys says, reaching across the table and taking my hand. "It is not the life she imagined, but she's making the best of it."

That sounds like me, in a way. This is not the life that I imagined at all, but I'm figuring it out. And I'm going to take it a step further. "I want you to teach me to use the magic."

He smiles, eyes suddenly bright with interest. "I'd be happy to."

"I'm done being helpless. If—when Ariana comes for me again, I'm not going to hide behind someone else. I'm not going to run. I need to be able to fight her."

"It will take practice. You won't be brilliant overnight—though I don't doubt you'll pick it up quickly."

I smirk, standing and assuming what might be a ready stance. "I seem to have a lot of time on my hands."

"And you're going to need every second of it if that's the way you make yourself ready," Aeric says from behind me. I whirl and find him standing in the door to the kitchen, my other mates behind him. "You can do better?" I ask, intentionally teasing him. "Prove it."

He strides across the room and kicks my feet wider apart, gently pressing my shoulders so that my knees bend, and position my hands more defensively. "It's a start."

"A good start," Kent says from behind as he pulls me into a hug that's full of relief. "But don't forget that I've still got moves that can take him down."

"Not for long." Aeric says smugly. "I'm going to learn it."

Urien leans between them and kisses me softly. "Are you all right?"

"I'm ready for answers," I say. "Did you find anything? *Anything?*"

"Yes and no." Brae slides into a chair near Verys, and he looks exhausted. "I tracked the source of the magic as far as I could. They used their own series of decoys. It wasn't Ariana who set the fire, it was someone she was controlling. They were already dead when I found them."

"She killed them?"

Brae scrubs a hand across his face. "She knew that we would find him. Covering her tracks."

Frustration grows in my chest. "But that tells us nothing."

"Not necessarily," Urien says. "It tells us that she doesn't trust her people. Or her control over them. It tells us that she's being careful for a reason, which means she probably has some kind of long-term plan."

"How does that help if we have no idea what the plan is?"

"It's a start," Brae says. "Because we know that whatever the plan is involves you."

I sit down again, my resolve waning. "She's just trying to kill me."

"Is she?" Aeric says, leaning against the doorframe. He's back in fae clothing and I'm distracted by the tightness of his shirt. I wonder if he heard Verys and I last night. I wonder what he thought and if he considered joining us.

In this exact moment I'm glad that none of our bonds are sealed. Because they would have felt the echo of that thought, and I don't think that we'd be talking about strategy anymore. In any case I have to make an effort to keep my eyes from drifting to Aeric's body. "She knew we were there. Either she had a spy, or she left magical traces in the store to tell her when we were there. We were in the store for at least an hour. Why not burn it then? Burning a store that she knows is empty doesn't benefit her."

Kent wraps his arms around my shoulders and presses a kiss to my neck as I try to put the pieces together. "So you think she knew we weren't there. If she knew, then why do it?"

"Exactly," Urien says. "Why burn down an empty building? Unless you're trying to send a message."

"Or get us to move where she wants us," Kent says. "Which she clearly wanted us to go home to her trap."

"It wasn't a very good trap," I say lightly. But nobody takes the bait. It could have gone very differently. They did take us by surprise. "If she doesn't want to kill me," I say. "Then what does she want?"

"No idea," Brae says. "But I think that's the right question to be asking."

There's something nagging at the edges of my mind, but it's not clear enough to see what it is yet. "She told me my magic was rare. That she needed it. And the Goddess said that she was stripped of her magic. Maybe since I didn't die, she wants more?"

Urien shrugs. "That's possible."

"That's what we need to know," I say. "What the hell is her goal and why does she need me to do it.

Just going after me doesn't solve anything—we already know that she isn't working alone."

Verys nods. "You're right."

Magic pulses under my skin, and for a second I feel like I see the puzzle clearly. But I can't hold onto it. Just the edges—which gives me an idea. An idea that they're going to hate and reject out of hand. But they'll have to get over that, because I don't see another way.

"You're not going to like this," I say.

Aeric rolls his eyes. "Safe to say none of us are going to like anything that starts with that sentence."

"We don't know where Ariana is. We don't know what her plan is. The only thing that we know is that she wants me, and we're not even sure if it's alive or dead. We have no leads on where to find her."

"You're right," Kent says, hands tightening on my shoulders. "I don't like this."

"We need to draw her out," I say. "Or I need to."

It takes a second to sink in, and then they're all talking at once, telling me absolutely no fucking way. Standing up, I wait for them to finish voicing their objections before I hold up a hand and they go quiet. None of them look happy, and if it weren't such a serious situation, I'd tease them for how identical they look in expression. Stern and moody and sexy.

"Tell me the other option," I say, looking at each of them in turn. "Seriously, I'm open to suggestions, but I don't see anything."

"There has to be something," Kent says.

"The only thing that's coming to mind is what we're already doing—running and hiding—and I am *done* with that."

"Kari," Urien says, taking a step closer and reaching for my hand. "Hiding isn't weak. It's keeping you alive."

I don't let him take my hand. Instead I cross my arms. "Yes. It's keeping me alive. And believe me when I say that I'm grateful for the way you all are trying to protect me. While we're here Verys is going to teach me to use this magic that I have, so I can defend myself, but I'm not going to turn into a warrior overnight. I know that. But running is only going to make her chase me. And I've already lost enough.

"I love you, and I want to spend my life with all of you. I don't want to spend it running and looking over my shoulder. So unless you guys have any other ideas, I'll be the bait."

Brae scrubs his hands over his face, leaning over and bracing his elbows on his knees. "I wish I had a better option. I don't."

"I don't want to have to do this," I say. "But I refuse to be helpless."

Kent wraps his arms around me from behind. "You've never been helpless."

"It feels that way," I say. "I need to take control of this. Please, don't be angry at me."

"No," Urien says. "Of course not. You're right."

The way Aeric is looking at me right now, I'm not sure that he agrees, but the tension in the room eases, and I feel like I can breathe. "Where should we set the trap?"

"Somewhere that Ariana would feel that she has the upper hand," Verys says. "Where she feels like she has the element of surprise."

"I'll find a place," Aeric says. "We can make sure there are wards that only activate when she enters so that she won't escape. We should see about getting you some kind of armor. Maybe Kaya will help."

"That would be perfect. I'd love to see her. And in the meantime I'll learn some magic." I say, sudden sadness filling me. "I wish you could all stay. Since the plan is me being bait, maybe we could all just go home? I promise I'll stay inside the wards."

"We need time to make the plan and execute it effectively. With the attack last night, it's safer for you to be somewhere Ariana is not aware of while we put it in place. And so far," Verys says, "There aren't any signs that she knows you're here."

It hadn't hit me how much I'd fallen into comfort living in the mansion with all of them until it's suddenly not an option. "I'll miss you."

Brae stands and pulls me close. "We can be here in moments. And I doubt any of us have the strength to stay away for long." He kisses me, letting his magic fall into me like a sunny wave. I don't want him to go, even though I know he has to. Verys and I staying here is already putting strain on his family, and I can't imagine what Darran might say or do if he found out that Verys invited four more males into his home.

I take a moment with each of them to say goodbye before they leave, intentionally using portals a distance away from the house so that the magic is less traceable.

Aeric is last. His hands are hard on my hips, pulling me firmly against his body. "If you're going to train, you *train*. I want you to be able to show me some badass moves."

I grin. "Maybe I'll even be able to take you down."

"I doubt that," he says, raising an eyebrow. He kisses me hard, stealing the last of my breath. "But I'm definitely going to enjoy feeling you try."

He's gone before I can ask him to stay a little

longer and show me exactly what he means. They all are, leaving me alone with Verys. I curl up with him, letting him hold me.

I wonder if this is always the way it will feel when we're apart. Will it be worse if our bonds are sealed? Whatever the case, I need a distraction. "When do we start?"

Verys brushes back my hair and tilts my chin up so I'm looking into his eyes. I'm not sure what he's looking for, but I hope he finds it. "How about right now?"

CHAPTER SEVENTEEN

KARI

We go out behind the house, onto that same hill that overlooks the city of the Lunar Court. A sharp wind is cutting across the plain, and I feel very awake. It reminds me of the depths of winter in New York, when some of the midtown streets become wind tunnels with freezing cold air that cuts through your clothes and makes you wonder why you live in a place that has that weather.

This is a little softer, but still cold. "Maybe you can teach me how to make the air around me warmer."

Verys smirks. "Maybe that would be a good reward. Or maybe I shouldn't. The cold could be a good motivator for you to learn quickly."

"I don't like to be cold," I say, narrowing my eyes and folding my arms over my chest.

"I'll warm you up later." I love the confidence and mischief on his face. Verys is fucking sexy, and I'm more than happy to let him warm me up wherever he likes.

I rub my arms to inject some warmth and shake my head. "Okay. Where do we start?"

"Start with what you did in New York," he says, squaring off across from me. "Just reach out."

When I reach for the magic, it's there and waiting. Fire and glitter and light and *heat*. Just holding it in my mind warms me, and I can't keep the grin off my face. That's awesome. I can be my own furnace.

It's not winter yet in the human world, and from what I've seen and been told, the weather is not strictly seasonal in Allwyn. So I haven't needed to bury myself in sweaters and blankets the way I usually do when winter rolls around. Now I may not even need to.

I use the same process I did at Lincoln Center—imagine holding a ball of that glittering gold in my hands, and pushing it away from myself, all the way to Verys. The magic collides with his chest and knocks against him. It's a strange sensation, feeling his body press against the magic, feeling *him*, but not touching him.

"Good," he says. "But you're forcing it."

"How can you tell?"

His own silvery magic curls around mine, and I can feel the twisting vibrations running back to me. "Because your reach is good, but that magic hit me like a battering ram. You pushed it out for the sake of pushing it out. Because I asked you to. But in order for magic to be used most effectively it has to be an extension of you."

I nod. That's the way it always felt when I pulled on that tiny thread of magic that I used in the shop. I was able to shape it with ease and instinct. And it should be the same concept here.

Dropping the image of the pile of magic in my hands, I try to figure out how that feels with this much magic. My own little sliver is an extension of myself, but I had to reach for it—straining to pull it from the depths of my gut.

I can still feel the thread of my personal magic floating through me. Smaller and delicate, and darker than the gold. It's more of a violet or blue, like the purest color of flame. But I don't have to reach for the Goddess's magic—my new magic—I still don't know how to identify it for myself. It rises to my fingertips almost before I have the chance to call it.

This time instead of holding it close to myself, I let it move with me. Moving my physical hand, it follows. I reach across the space between Verys and I and use the magic to touch him on the shoulder. It's so much easier this way, though I wouldn't have been able to put a finger on why if he hadn't explained it.

This feels more like inhaling and exhaling the magic like it's part of the oxygen around me, instead of trying to form the power into a shape like play dough.

"That's better," Verys says. "How does it feel?"

"Easier," I say. "I expected it to be harder."

He chuckles. "I won't say that it will be easy the whole time, but you definitely have an advantage because you've used magic before."

Thank the Goddess. I don't know how you would figure out how to shape any kind of power if you had never encountered it before. "I want to learn more than just defense. But I guess that's probably what we should start with."

"I agree. And for today, let's focus on stopping something physical—because that's easier than stopping a magical force."

"Really?" I pull my power back from him. "I would have thought the opposite."

He crosses to me and places his hands on my shoulders. "Even the strongest person has physical limitations. But magical limitations are harder to define, especially since we're dealing with someone who is actively trying to steal magic. She may have more power than we expect—the same way that you do."

Shit. That's true. I didn't even think about that. "Okay."

"Start slow," he says. "Push my hands away."

I try, and nothing happens. The sensation of Verys's hands is real, and I can feel it on my skin and with my power, but the magic seems to seep right through his hands. "Use your hands to get the motion right, but try not to touch me. You don't want to rely on the physical movement."

I press myself into him, enjoying the feeling of the way we fit together. "Why not?"

He doesn't miss a beat, and his face is entirely serious. "Because if you're in a situation where you need to defend yourself magically, there's every chance that you're going to need to do it physically too. And it's also likely those two things will be different."

Panic rises in my chest and I push it down. This was my idea. I can do this. But thinking about actually doing this—about being attacked again—makes my breath go short.

I push up with my hands, filling them with power, but stop short of grabbing his wrists. The magic is an extension of me. And I can visualize the glittering frameworks of it in my mind. They are my hands, but more than my hands.

Verys's hands lift off my shoulders an inch.

"They're heavy," I say. "Way heavier than your actual arms."

"It will feel that way," he says softly. "For a while. The larger the object, the more magic it requires. And the higher your level of focus and practice, the more you can do with less."

I let his hands fall, and they brush down my arms to my shoulders, adding an entirely different type of warmth to me. "That's how you've been able to do so much with so little?"

He nods, letting his arms slide around me more, until I'm sealed around his body and our faces are close. "Yes. And I've had a lot of time to practice. Now that I have more to work with, I have more work to do."

I'm distracted by his closeness, and the way his fingers are pressing into my back. He tilts his head down to mine, a faint smile playing on his lips. "Stop me from kissing you."

"I don't want to do that."

"Try," he smirks. "It takes more focus to resist something that you want."

At first I just push out with my magic, but it skims off him like a pebble skipping on a pond. He's leaning closer, and the way he's looking at me with lust in his eyes and promises of more makes me want to abandon the mission. But I don't. I call the magic, and let it fill my entire body until I'm nothing but a being of sparkling gold, and I push.

I manage to stop him from leaning closer, freezing him in time. But his arms are still around me, drifting down my back towards my ass. *Off*, I think the word.

Nothing.

I focus, envisioning the magic become sharp and hard like a shell, and I shout it in my mind. *OFF!*

The magic blows outwards with a snap. And Verys's arms fall from around my waist and he takes a step back. Now he's beaming. The force of the magic isn't much compared to some that I've felt before, and the power contracts back into me immediately. But I did it. "How was that?"

This time when he kisses me I don't stop him, and I can read the approval in his kiss. For not having had any practice, Verys is a *damn* good kisser. With the dedication he's had to being celibate and making do without magic, I know that he's only going to get better with time. That's the thought that makes me shiver with want. Because if he's already this good, Verys a year from now is going to wreck me.

Goddess, I want him to wreck me.

"That was very good," he says, holding me close

again. "You're going to feel the effects in a few seconds."

"What?" Right after I say that, I feel it hit me. Swooning weakness that strikes me in the knees and the rest of my limbs, and I sag against him. "Woah."

"There it is," he laughs. "You're not used to expending power like that, and it's not like sex and Carnal power where the magic you expend is given back to you. With more experience, you'll feel the effects less."

"This is why the three of you tried to preserve your magic on the trip." I feel weak and a little depleted. But even now the magic is building back up. How much magic did the Goddess give me? Is there an infinite supply? If I run out is that the end of it? How do I recharge it if I'm low?

The true weakness only lasts for about a minute before my body doesn't feel like jelly and I can once again carry my own weight. "That feels the way I used to feel after a full day of dancing. And not easy dancing."

"I would imagine. We're going to have to test your limits. But not now."

"Why not?"

"I want to see how you react to using magic. Training is important, but making sure you can survive the training is equally important. Would you like to see the city?"

"I can do more."

He chuckles and leads me towards the house. "There will be plenty more, believe me. You're not done for the day. I'm tempted to take the next training session to our bedroom."

"I don't think that I'm going to do much learning while I'm naked."

That cocky smirk that's new to his face but that I'm learning to love crosses his face. "On the contrary," he says. "You need to be able to defend yourself even if you're naked. *Especially* if you're naked."

The eagerness in his voice makes me wonder what exactly he has planned. This is Verys unrestrained. For the first time in I'm not even sure how long he's not holding a part of himself back, and it's beautiful. And I'm absolutely sure that he's going to accomplish the goal of helping me use my magic, even if he has to use my own desire against me.

That thought draws me between anxiety and anticipation. If he tells me to push him away when he's in the middle of pleasuring me, I don't know that I'll be able to to do it.

But there's a part of me that's curious to find out.

"What will we do in the city?" I ask as we cross

through the courtyard of the house and out the beautiful front that I have only seen in the moonlight.

"Maybe see Kaya?"

"We can send her a message?"

Verys takes my hand. "Just like human cities, the courts have evolved in commerce and specialties. Though it doesn't quite compare to the artistic courts, the Lunar Court has established itself as an excellent place for textiles. After meeting Kaya I'm sure there are shops that will know her, and that she'll be excited to visit."

I'd like that. Kaya's vibrant energy sounds like something that I could very much embrace right now.

We walk down the hill in the wind, and it strikes me how different the Lunar Court appears from the Carnal Court the Crystal Court. Every Court I've seen before has been wildly different. Far more diverse than anything in the human realm.

Unsurprising since it's Lunar, but the landscape in front of me is stark and the road is made of fine white powder that curls up under my feet as we walk. It looks like the moon might, with everything shining in pale monochrome.

The few trees that I can see look like what might be birch trees on earth, but shot through with shining silver and glittering white with gilded leaves. They shimmer in the near constant wind.

Unlike the other cities I've seen though, the Lunar Court doesn't have walls. The buildings on the outer edges of the city are tall to shield the city from the wind, but also to allow it to pass through in places. The architecture is all clean lines and simple shapes, very unlike the colorful chaos and intricate details of the Crystal Court.

A thought hits me. "You said it was safer for me to be in a place where we were sure Ariana didn't know about."

Verys nods. "Yes."

"So wouldn't it be safer for me not to be seen?"

He slows a step. "Yes."

"So we're already using me as bait, to see if we're actually safe here." I smirk at him. "Clever."

He laughs. "I knew you would figure it out. I don't have any expectations of being in danger here, but if we are, I'd rather know sooner than later."

We pass a building that is clearly the temple, in what seems to be at the exact center of the city, with large avenues emerging from the plaza like the spokes of a wheel. The temple is unlike the others that I've seen—it's circular like the plaza, with tall columns lining the edge and holding up one massive stone ring. It makes sense, leaving it open to the sky so they can see the moon.

At a distance, I can see the statue of the Goddess in the center of the columns. The magic inside me unfurls and releases perfect warmth, as if in recognition.

The central plaza is filled with the commerce I've grown used to seeing in the cities, and like Verys said, a lot of them are stalls that contain cloth. Beautiful cloth in every shade and glimmer that I could imagine and more.

Verys makes a motion with his hand, and there's a series of glowing symbols that quickly disappear into the air and vanish. "What was that?"

"Our message."

"Will you teach me how to do that?"

Taking my hand, he spins me under his arm like we're dancing and pulls me in. "I'll teach you everything."

"If you two need a room I can come back," a loud voice says behind me. "Otherwise I'm here to make you look fabulous."

When I turn around, Kaya is standing there, striking a pose far more dramatic than is needed. It suits her perfectly. She's smirking. "Miss me?"

CHAPTER EIGHTEEN

KARI

Kaya is just as crazy and vibrant as I remember. Her bright red hair stands out against the background of mostly pale buildings. As soon as I see her she approaches and wraps me in a massive hug. "I should absolutely skin you alive for not sending me a message sooner," she says. "I've been wanting to hear how you love your closet!"

I laugh as she practically crushes me with her hug. "I'm sorry. It's been a little crazy."

"Tell me everything. And while you do, we're going to pick some amazing fabric so I can make you clothes you're not going to want to take off even with five delicious men begging to have you naked."

I very much pretend that I'm not blushing from head to toe. "If you imagine that's what's happening, you're very mistaken."

Kaya slings her arm around my shoulder. "I'm very not. Now what am I making you? I realized I didn't send you any lingerie which I admit was a bit of an oversight."

"We were hoping you could make me clothes that are armored."

Her eyebrows raise into her hairline. "Seems like you have some things to tell me."

"You could say that."

Verys keeps watch behind us while Kaya marches me through the market with comfort and ease. She's been here before. And just like with Emma and Odette, I tell her everything while she's picking out fabrics while barely consulting me. Rich colors and some lighter ones.

I particularly love a pale grey that she's picked out. It shines like a pearl and is so soft I feel like I can't stop touching it. I never really thought I could pull off grey with my coloring, so I'm happy.

She shakes her head when I've finished the story. "I don't know what you did to attract Allwyn's attention, girl. But I understand why you need armor. I have everything we need for the moment. But these are going to need more than just me taking your measurements by eye, and time to weave wards."

"You can come with us," Verys says. Instead of us walking all the way back to the house, he simply opens a portal that's directly into the bedroom we're sharing in his mother's home. That's something I need to learn how to do because the amount of time saved with portals is blowing my mind.

Back when I danced, if I had been able to do that I would have slept as late as possible and then portaled myself directly into company class.

We step through the rip in space and the world goes fuzzy and dizzy for a second before everything snaps into focus again. Almost immediately Kaya spreads the fabric she's retrieved all over the bed and begins to sort through it.

"Now, how much have you learned?" She asks as she picks up the grey fabric.

"Magically?" She nods. "I only just started before we met up with you."

"Has she rested enough, Verys?"

I cross my arms and stare her down. "If you're planning on making me stop you from stabbing me with a pin, no dice."

Kaya laughs and rolls her eyes. "No. But I was going to have you practice forming a shield."

"She should be fine," Verys says.

Kaya points to a spot on the floor. "Stand here so I can work on you. And while you do that, form a shield around yourself. Verys can throw some things at you and you can stop them."

I shake my head. "How am I supposed to do that?"

"It'll be different for every person," she says lightly. "So I can't just tell you how to do it. But the idea is that you can just have the shield in place around you to stop physical and magical attacks."

I roll my eyes. "Completely simple."

Settling in a chair in the corner, Verys chuckles. "It's a good thing to practice, and we'll start lightly. Just give it a try."

A shield. From all angles. I don't need a specific image, I just need a bubble. Reaching for the magic, I let it bubble up and I let it expand around me like a bubble. Not pushing it away but extension. Almost like a cocoon. Silver magic threads along the edges of the shield, and for all the world it feels like Verys is running his fingers across my skin. "That's nice," he murmurs.

Kaya's magic isn't as gentle. The fiery red magic fizzles across the shield and I jump. "Not at all bad for a first try. Arms up."

She goes to work with the fabric, measuring it against me in ways that I'm sure make sense to her. Verys pushes harder. And the magic flexes like a bubble but doesn't burst. "Do I need actually protect against magic?"

"Of course," Verys and Kaya say at the same time, and I laugh. "But the Goddess told me the magic would protect my mind from invasion. So I don't have to worry about anybody…magically hypnotizing me or anything."

"You think that's the only thing you can do to a person with magic?"

I've never seen anything else, but I suppose I haven't seen very much. Kaya is quiet, her face troubled as she glances at Verys. "Fae combat is not like human combat," he says quietly. "We do not need weapons. Not when we can move our fingers and slice the enemy in half." The magic he's brushing along my bubble turns sharp enough to steal my breath, and with one fierce blow the shield shatters into nothing. "Again." He says.

I wrap magic around me like a blanket. Thicker and more solid. I don't feel an end of the power—a seemingly infinite well to pull from. Verys's magic crashes against it like a wave, and it crumbles into thin air. "Again." He stands from his chair and takes a step towards me. And I know what he's trying to do. In this moment he's no longer my lover and friend—he's the person hunting me, and as slowly as he's moving he'll reach me in moments. The fae trying to take me will grant me even less time.

I pull up more magic and abandon the attempt to circle myself completely and throw it up in a wall in front of me. Moving so fast I almost feel the wind whipping past my cheek his magic spins around me and cracks into the shield from behind, slithering past my skin and intentionally brushing me. "Again, Kari. Keep me out."

My lungs feel like they can't contract, iron bands around my chest. I'm panicking. Just like I would if someone were coming at me, and I can't afford to panic. *Get your shit together, Kari.* I'm resisting the full magic. I can sense it there under the surface, like one of those holes in the ocean that you can't tell the depth, and I'm afraid that I might lose myself. Like I did the first time. I couldn't find my way back to my body and that is absolutely terrifying.

But if I don't, I won't be able to defend myself.

Falling one way or the other tangles all the strings.

This is one of those moments. I can choose to embrace this magic and what it means, or I can reject it entirely. But it has to be now. I've been avoiding it and trying not to think about it. I meant what I said to them. I'm done hiding and I'm ready, but that doesn't make taking this step feel any less like stepping off a cliff into nothing.

There's a sense of something bigger, outside of myself. Like this is a knot in that tangle, with paths branching outward, and Allwyn waiting for me to choose. The whole world has held its breath, and me along with it.

Choose. I hear the musical voice in my head.

There's no judgement or tone to tell me which choice would be better. Only kindness and understanding for whatever way I choose to break. *Choose.*

In the end it doesn't feel like a choice. I'm not giving up, and fear is something that I've had enough of. Closing my eyes, I open myself to the magic. If before I was dipping my toe in a puddle, this is opening the floodgates. It presses against the edges of me, barely contained, and if I needed it, there's more.

I barely have to think to let it surround me—it wants to. I'm controlling it, but it already knows what I want and it's taking shape, hardening around me. I'm sleeping beauty encased in glass, and this time when Verys's magic comes for me it glances off the facets of the shield like nothing. His magic beats against mine, collapsing in wave after wave that I barely feel. I am an island—untouchable. I am myself, and I am more than myself.

When I open my eyes, the entire room is bathed in golden light, the shield around me entirely visible, separating me from Verys with a barrier drenched in radiance. His hands are pressed to the barrier, and his face is a mix of awe and concern. It's easy to let him in and keep the shield in place.

I watch, seemingly at a distance as his hands sink

through the magic and the rest of him follows. He's safe now too. I'll protect him. Or we'll protect each other. He adds his magic to the shield, gilding it with silver and shivering vibrations.

His lips fall onto mine with a force I've never felt from him, and I'm slammed back into myself. I'm in control and the magic didn't overtake me. I'm *here*. And Verys's magic twisting with mine sends need piercing through my veins. I need him closer, faster.

"Exactly like that," he whispers. "Keep everyone out. Even me. Even us."

"I don't want you out," I murmur against his mouth. "I want you in."

"I think that's my cue to go," Kaya says from behind me, voice barely containing her amusement.

I startle, having completely forgotten she was in the room. "I'm so sorry, Kaya."

"Why?" She lifts an eyebrow. "The only thing you should apologize for is making me jealous of the fun the two of you are about to have." The blush takes over my whole body, which only makes her laugh harder. When she raises her hand to the edge of the shield, I consciously note to let her in, and Kaya's is beaming as she steps through the barrier and pulls me into a hug. "That was amazing. Keep practicing, because none of us want to lose you. I'll send the clothes as soon as they're finished!"

She's disappeared into a portal almost before I can track her, all the cloth with her. "I didn't mean to scare her away," I say.

Verys pulls my face back to his, not missing a beat with his next kiss. "You didn't scare her, she's just observant and realized what's about to happen." He nudges me backwards and as soon as I lose my balance on the edge of the bed he falls with me, pulling me on top of him.

"What's about to happen?"

Lips drag down my neck, causing shivers all the way down to my toes. The magic surrounding me has faded back to invisible, but it's still there, twisting and pulsing and keeping everything out but the two of us. "I could tell you in detail, just how thoroughly I'm about to fuck you." he says, letting his words and breath drift little eddies of power across my skin. Power created with the express purpose of seeking out my core. It finds my desire and drives it higher until I'm panting for him. Clinging to his body, already about to come just from the sheer force of this need. "Or, I could just show you."

He rolls us together so his body is pressing into mine. His clothes do nothing to mask his own desire, pressing hard between us. Goddess, yes.

"Show me," I beg. "Please."

He smiles down at me, kissing along my jaw with agonizing slowness. And I don't think this time it's about exploration—I just think that Verys enjoys taking his time. And drawing out both our pleasure as long as is possible. I love it, hate it, and crave the depth of it.

"I have only one condition."

"Oh?" I'm barely focused on his words and entirely distracted by the hand that's slipping below the waistband of my jeans to tease me. I'm already soaking wet and when he touches me, he only smiles wider.

"Keep that shield up."

"No promises." I say. So far the magic seems steady, but when I'm lost in orgasm I don't think I'll have enough brain power to keep it going.

Verys rises up on his knees, towering above me. "Yes," he says. "Promise. Or I might have to reconsider."

He's still smiling, so I know he's not entirely serious. But it doesn't look like he's joking either. "Are you saying that you won't have sex with me if I can't keep up the shield?"

"No," he says, grinning. "I'm definitely going to fuck you. But if the shield falls, I'm not going to let you orgasm until the shield is up again."

"You're blackmailing my orgasms?"

He kisses me lightly. "Yes."

"I think that's a little unnecessary."

He chuckles and presses a kiss to my lips. "And I think it's brilliant. I think Aeric would approve of the training method."

"Aeric isn't here," I mutter. His hand sinks beneath my waistband again, and I gasp, the magic at the tips of his fingers ripples into me and ignites. Pleasure splinters through me with a snap, and I arch up to meet him, voice lost in a moan. "Fucking hell."

"Fucking hell is about right," he says, stripping out of his clothes. "You have no idea how incredible you look when you come. Even if you have far too many clothes on."

"That's your fault."

"True, but the rest is yours." He helps me out of my pants and peels the shirt over my head. I would do it but my bones are still jelly due to his clever fingers. "Where's your shield?"

Shit. The magic isn't wrapped around us anymore. I lost it, just like I thought I might. And I don't have a chance to pull it back, because Verys lines himself up with me, and in one thrust he's too deep inside me that I can't breathe. "Oh Goddess."

He laughs softly. "Get your shield back, Kari."

I shake my head back and forth, biting my lip as he thrusts. He's already sent me over once, and after the first orgasm they like to keep coming. "How can you possibly expect me to do that right now?"

He thrusts deep, that unnameable ecstasy sinking through me like sand. Silver hair cascades around my face, and he leans close. "I expect you to do it whenever it's needed so that you can keep yourself alive."

He thrusts again, this time piercing me with magic too, and I cry out, my voice echoing off the walls. My magic catches his and it makes everything *more*. I can't breathe, can't focus on anything but the friction of his cock as he drives into me. "I can't."

"You can," he says. And suddenly he's moving slower.

"Don't hold back on my account," I say desperately. "You've got a lot of lost orgasms to make up for."

Verys smirks at me, settling between my legs comfortably so that I'm stuffed full of him but he's barely moving. It's driving me mad. "I've got a century's worth of patience on that front, mate." The roughness in his voice tells me that he's just as turned on as I am. But there's a determination in his eyes that can't be doubted. He won't let himself—or me—come until the shield is back in place.

I grab his shoulders to steady myself and focus on his eyes as I reach for the magic. Goddess, it only makes it worse. My magic explodes with his, and I can barely control the impulse to just fall into climax and forget what he's asked of me. But I don't want to disappoint him. One breath, and then another. Again. Until I'm filled to the brim with both him and with power and that shell is surrounding the two of us. I thicken and harden the shell until I'm sure that absolutely nothing will get through. "Good," he says. "Now don't lose it."

"You're killing me."

He smiles. An expression with an edge to it. "I would never. You're my mate." And he lets himself go. The devastating wave of bliss hits me a second later and I let it wash over me, my cries lost in Verys covering my mouth with his. Gold meets silver inside my soul, and what was already never-ending seems to grow and expand. It's not a hardship to hold onto the shield. I don't even have to think. The magic is a part of me, and it acts for me. All I have to do is enjoy my mate.

And oh, I do.

When he releases my lips, I smirk up at him. "How was that?"

"Perfect."

"So no more holding back orgasms?"

He chuckles. "I wouldn't dream of it."

"Good." I tilt my hips up to his and pull him down to me again, and I let myself get thoroughly lost in him.

CHAPTER NINETEEN

KARI

The better part of a week flies by in the same way. Training and sex. It's almost easy to ignore the fact that there's something big hanging over my head. But there haven't been any signs of Ariana's presence here.

I spend the mornings with Siona in the kitchen, and she tells me stories about Verys when he was younger. It gives me a chance to know him in a completely different light. My favorite story so far is that Verys rescued a fae beast when he was still a child. Somehow the beast—in the form of a rabbit—had become injured and lost on the plains of the Lunar court. Maybe a predator, or maybe something darker had had its way with it.

Verys found the creature on his way home and brought it with him. And he put every ounce of care and magic he could into caring for the creature until it was well. And though she made sure that he was not near when she told me the next part, he shed a few tears when he had to release the creature. And it did come back to visit from time to time. Though it stopped after it figured out that Verys no longer lived here.

There are other stories too. Funny ones of mishaps both magical and not. And more harrowing stories of the last fae war—the first and last great conflict in Allwyn since Cerys created it—when Siona was almost sure that Verys was going to die. I hope to meet every one of my mate's families if I can get to know them like this. Now, when I look at Verys, I see more than I already did.

When he meets my eyes my heart goes silent in my chest for a moment, and I ache for all the pain he has been dealt in his life, and I hope that I can ease some of that pain.

In the afternoons we train together, and Verys takes it as an opportunity to show me the Lunar lands. We take portals to some places that are both beautiful and stark. A lake of bright, milky blue that stands out against the pale dust that seems to cover the ground everywhere. And the lake is hot, of all things. The steam rising into the sky, which varies in color from that same beautiful blue to a lavender and back through a pearly grey.

There are mountains on the outskirts of the court that rise with abrupt magnitude. These are nothing like the mountains on earth that I've seen. These would dwarf those in a heartbeat. Snow—or maybe dust—brushes the tops of them that fade into the sky, so far up they're difficult to see. The landscapes not only provide a gorgeous landscape for the training, they help my focus. I have to keep working with my power in unfamiliar environments, and I'm getting better.

Not good, but better.

I can now hold the shield almost without thinking about it, and Verys makes me do it at all times. The only time I can't consciously do it is when I'm sleeping. But this power inside me works with me the more I practice. And I'm not entirely sure if it's just the way that this works, or if it's because this was a gift and not entirely mine. But the shield has been intact the past couple of days when I've woken, draped over Verys and I, because inevitably we're tangled together.

That's how the training always ends. Verys has to push me hard. We've progressed from shielding to fighting back and more. I can keep him away from me, and his magic. He's hurled rocks at the shield, starting small, and growing until there was a rock that was as tall as I was. I knew that if the shield had failed, he still had a hold on it—he would never have let it hit me. But the shield cracked it in half.

Turning the magic around and striking out is much harder, especially when I'm trying to keep the shield in place too. Even shielding while running and dodging is easier than trying to actively attack. Not to mention that I don't particularly like striking out at Verys. Which he shoved aside with a smirk, saying that he's been doing it for days and it's still giving him tiny heart attacks.

Fair is fair.

But at the end of the day, after having had to treat each other like enemies, and feeling each other's power, we barely make it back to the bed. Every encounter gives Verys more confidence, and I was exactly right that he's learning and growing and I think he might know what makes my body tick more than I do now.

And tick it does. The minute he touches me in that slow, deliberate way that makes me shiver I'm instantly wet and wanting, and he's more than happy to oblige. I even managed to get him to let me taste him again, with the promise that we weren't sealing the bond. It didn't last long before he hauled me off my knees and back to the bed so he could bury himself to the hilt inside me. I love that I'm his first everything. And it makes me want to give him a first too. I've been thinking about it, but I have yet to ask.

As delicious as every moment has been, after so many days, I miss my other mates too. Even though it still feels strange to want so many people at once.

I've seen them in tiny doses, dropping in for a few minutes here and there as they make their plans. But those visits have barely been long enough for a kiss. Not long enough for a true conversation or anything further.

I miss Brae's steadiness and insight. I miss Aeric's fierce passion. Kent's firm sweetness and Urien's gentle practicality. Siona's hospitality has been lovely, and this place is beautiful, but I want to go home. This week has cemented that the Carnal Court is my home now. Whenever I think the word home, that's the place I imagine, along with the warm feeling I've always associated with the word.

I'm looking forward to going back, and I think Verys is too. In the time we've been here, I've seen Darran maybe twice, and both times he was brusque and unfriendly. I'm not a fan. But he hasn't said anything yet that's made me need to punch him in the face, so we're in a peaceful stalemate. Verys laughed when I told him that I would be willing to punch his stepfather. I don't think he believed that I was serious.

I am.

In the bedroom we've been sharing, I pull on one of the things that Kaya sent for me. She's outdone herself as usual—clothes that fit me perfectly and are beautiful and stylish and warded to the teeth. I don't have enough experience yet to discern the individual spells, but I can feel the wards buzzing faintly under my fingers when I brush them across the fabric. And because it's Kaya, she included both a ballgown which I can't imagine myself wearing when I need armor, and more sets of lingerie and nightgowns than I could ever need.

I laughed, but I have been wearing them—at least until my clothes come off. There are worse things than having an extra layer of protection while you sleep. And I know all of my mates agree, even if I would much rather sleep skin-on-skin.

The soft grey pants I pull on have quickly become some of my favorites. I love them so much I'm probably going to ask her to make me more in this style. I never thought I would have a personal stylist, but I can't say that I'm complaining. These have a high waist with six buttons, vaguely military in style with a little bit of a flare in the leg. They're perfect. I pair it with a burgundy shirt with sleeves just past the elbow. How she manages to capture my need for comfort but make it look like I stepped out of a store on Fifth Avenue I'll never understand, but I need to get this woman to New York.

New York Fashion Week will never be the same.

"Where are we going today?" I ask Verys.

He reaches for my hand as he draws a line in the

air and crimson light splits it open. "It's a surprise. Eyes closed." I raise an eyebrow, but I close my eyes. He guides me through the portal and I feel that familiar sense of dizziness as I'm transported from one place to another. It's even colder than I was expecting when we step through, and I reach for my magic instinctively now, and it banishes the cold instantly. Amazing how after such a short time it's become second nature to have this level of magic. I'm not surprised that humans are jealous of fae in the slightest. Having this kind of flexibility at your fingertips is fucking awesome.

"All right, you may open your eyes."

We're in the mountains, not just seeing them from a distance. From what it looks like, we've stepped out into the valley between peaks, on the shores of a tiny lake that's perfectly smooth despite the wind and shimmers like a moonstone. The peaks on either side of us tower into the invisible distance above, and when we're this close, I can see the changing colors of the rocks. Huge streaks of rusted orange and vibrant yellow along with the blacks and browns I would expect of stone. It's the most color in the landscape I've seen in this court.

Some of those pale petrified trees dot the edge of the lake, casting long shadows across the water. The image is entirely alien, and by far the most beautiful place that I've seen in the Lunar Court. "Wow."

"I thought you might like this place."

"What are we working on today? The more beautiful place, the more I think you're trying to distract me."

Verys's face is grim. "Unfortunately yes. And you'll have some other distractions as well."

"Mind if we join you?"

I turn to find the rest of my mates stepping out of a portal, and I can't keep the smile off my face. "We're going to train together?"

Aeric reaches me first, dipping me back into a sweeping kiss that melts my knees. "Verys told us that you're progressing well and need a bit of a challenge. We thought we could help."

"I'd like that," I breathe. Kent takes my hand and stands beside me as I look back at Verys. "What did you have in mind?"

His demeanor hasn't lightened. "Ariana seems intent on taking you. Getting you elsewhere. She's not a fool, so there's every chance that she'll send more than one person after you. Or come herself with an accomplice."

Oh. He wanted me to practice defending myself against multiple people. I'm not perfect at any of this, and I won't be for a long time. I don't have a hundred years of muscle and mental memory. But the idea is that I get good enough that I can hold my own until help arrives. Until this is all over—however it ends—I'm not going to be alone for long. "Okay. What should I do?"

The five of them arrange themselves in a loose circle around me. "Just magic first," Verys says. "Make sure we can't get through."

I can do that. Filling the shield with power feels like a reflex now, and I strengthen it just as I feel a stab from Aeric's spicy green magic. He's not holding back. Nor should he. I need this to be as real as possible. I force more power into the shield where he presses in, and am nearly distracted enough that when Urien slices across my back that the barrier shakes.

Brae's assault is slow and steady pressure that would flatten me if I didn't keep powering more charging into the barricade. More hits, scattered like stars from Verys. Again, again, and again. Their magic is like a battering ram against the shield. It's both exhilarating and exhausting but nothing gets through.

"Kari," Verys says. "Keep Kent out."

Fuck. I'm barely keeping up with the onslaught of magic, I haven't even been paying attention to what's actually around me. I have to turn to find

Kent, and he's already closer than I expect him to be. He strides forward with determination. I know that he'd die before he would ever hurt me, but I understand how he was able to be a cop. If he were coming after me like this for real, I'd already be running.

He slams into the bubble I'm holding, and I feel it waver. The invisible attacks haven't stopped, but Kent keeps trying. I take a step back, and another, and it feels like so much. Kent presses his shoulder against the glittering wall that's become visible as I put all of my attention on it, and he shoves his entire weight into it. It's fine. I'm holding it.

And then the rest of them strike at once. Magic strikes the shield all together, and the ripples from that one attack are too much. The pressure Kent's causing cracks it, and I trip backwards. Kent is already moving, catching me before I smack my head on the rocky shore, and breathing heavily. "Are you all right?"

I nod. "Yeah, I think so." More faces appear above mine. "I'm sorry," I say. "I wasn't expecting that kind of coordination."

Urien snorts indelicately, which is so unlike him that it makes me laugh. "Kari, that was incredibly impressive. Even accounting for the amount of power you've been given, holding off the magic of four fae warriors while being attacked is no small thing."

"Really?"

Verys makes a face. "She hasn't believed me once when I've told her that she's doing well."

Reaching down and grasping one of my hands, Brae assists Kent in helping me to my feet. "They're right that was very good."

"It was," Aeric says. "And we should do it again. And you should try to fight back."

I wince. "I'm having trouble with that part. I don't want to hurt any of you."

He steps closer to me, just like when he told me to make sure that I was training my ass off. He takes my face in his hands, and his features and green skin and eyes look so vibrant here against the pale backdrop. Full of life and passion. "We can handle what you unleash, Kari. And that's what you need to do. You need to let go and know what it feels like to *unleash hell*. It's not something you want to do for the first time in combat. You should do it where you're safe. This is the place. Fight back."

My heart pounds at his words. The way he says them, like he has no doubt that I can do that, just let fury and danger come pouring out of my skin like it's easy. "It's not that simple."

"Yes it is," he says, putting his palm gently on my

chest. "You're angry. You're grieving. You've had enough. Let it all go. Here and now. Give in and fight back." I hesitate, and he keeps going. "You stopped being bound by human ideas of politeness the moment you were attacked. And the fae coming after you *will not give you the same consideration.* Please, Kari," his voice is softer now, pressing softly with his palm. "Show me what's here."

I look around at the rest of my men, standing close enough to hear his words, and every one gives a sign of agreement. They believe in me. They think that I can do this. I thought that I had given in—given everything. But it's not true.

"Okay."

Aeric smiles, just a little. "I love you. Don't hold back."

I nod as they back up, returning to their circle. But this is different. They're moving. They're not going to just use magic this time. I have to stop them.

My shield is barely in place before the first magic drops down on me like a fist. Fuck. Little taps on the barrier behind me to distract me and another slice to the front. Kent is already approaching the shield, so I make it stronger. And stronger still. But he's backing me up.

I stagger forward towards him from a sudden

physical blow to the back of my shield, and I whirl on instinct, magic following and forcing Urien to back up. Verys lifts a stone, and uses his own power to propel it towards me, and I shove it away before it even has a chance to shatter on the shield.

Behind me I can feel Brae move with a bar of power in his hand, aiming to pierce the shield. I turn over my shoulder and use extra power to hold him back, not letting him any closer. That's when I feel Kent running at me again. I can *feel* him.

With just Verys, it was easy to focus on him. With so many people I have to rely on the magic to tell me what I can't see, and it does as if I had consciously asked it to do that. *I can trust this.* Something settles in my chest, like fitting in that final elusive piece of a jigsaw puzzle. I just have to let it be.

A hailstorm of power and stones flies at me from the left, and the pieces of jagged rock disintegrate in front of me. That's what they'll do, if they find me. If *she* finds me. They'll toy with me until I'm so tired that I can't fight them off again. Wear me down.

Let it all go.

Enough. I've had enough.

The anger I've been avoiding rises up in my chest like a crimson flood. Every moment of feeling helpless and afraid. Every time I've had to run away or lost something precious to me. Aeric shoots a blast of green power that's so strong I can feel the shield cracking under the pressure. No.

I fall back into the power. *My* power. I seal the cracks and send my own blast of fire towards him, not looking to see where it landed because the others are still attacking. Still pressing. But I can feel them now, every move and intention. It's like a dance, blocking and pushing back and holding them still.

The fae are not going to give up. I can see it in their eyes. Kent too, is standing outside the shield, breathing hard. He'll do what he can without magic. Aeric looks at me, and I can almost hear the words he said to me.

Here and now. Let it all go.

Verys is the first one to move. There's a sword in his hand formed of silver magic, shining in the bright. And the other fae follow him. Swords form in their hands of pure power, and as one they approach the shield. I don't see the faces of my mates. Instead I see Ariana's face as she laughed at me. As she looked down on me while I was dying. I see the hooded figures that stalked us with birds and poison. The fae that bound me so that Ariana could take my life.

I see my sixth mate, hatred in his eyes as he tries to break through everything to get to me. And pain greater than I've ever felt cracks through my chest along with this anger. No. Tears well in my eyes and spill over as I let in the power. I am nothing but a cascade of stars, consumed by fire and fury. The power moves with me or I move with it, but it doesn't matter. With this much power it's only the spark that matters, and that's the end.

I am a supernova. Nothing will touch me.

Then I unleash everything.

Power flows outward, pouring forth from fissures so deep in this world I will never know the bottom. It is so bright that I have to close my eyes and my throat is raw from screaming. One single blast, and I know that I could tear the world apart if I wanted to. That anger is just the kindling for a rage that is not entirely my own, and I let it out into the atmosphere.

It rings off the mountains and scorches the trees, leaving marks that will never fade.

And then it's over.

Light flickers and fades into nothing and I can see that I'm standing at the center of nothing. Stones and sand and dust have blown outward from me. Trees are broken, boulders cracked, and not one of my mates is upright. They're scattered around me, and for a moment I feel the shock of horror before Verys is the one who moves. He looks at me in awe, and then the others do to.

Brae is the closest, and grips my arms and pulls me against him hard. "Yes," is all he says before he consumes me.

I barely have a chance to speak before I'm pulled away by Kent. "Did I hurt any of you?"

"No," Verys says. "But that was what you needed."

"I don't know how I did it."

Aeric's hand curves around the back of my neck and guides my gaze to his. "Yes, you do."

He's right. And I'm not sure I'll ever be able to do that again. That amount of anger and grief, it's too much. "I don't want to have to," I say, shaking my head.

"Believe me," Urien says. "We don't want you to have to either."

"But if your life is in danger," Kent says softly. "Then that's exactly what you do."

Brae chuckles. "Though even before that you were holding your own. Once we teach you to fight, you'll be a force to be reckoned with."

I let my head fall against Aeric's chest. "Not today," I say. "Please."

"No, not today."

The familiar exhaustion from the use of so much power sets in, and I nearly fall. It's gotten much better, but that was more than I've ever used.

Thankfully it's only after I stop and breathe that the weakness seems to set in.

"Let's get you back," Verys says.

"Can you all stay?" I ask, hopefully.

There's a pause. I don't look up, I know they're communicating silently. "Yes," Kent answers. "We can stay."

Which is how I end up back in the bedroom, my head pillowed on Aeric's chest and my feet in Kent's lap. Brae at my back and Urien close by. Verys observes, and smiles when I meet his eyes. He's not bothered in the slightest, given how much time we've spent wrapped up in each other. And I want the rest of them too. But this exhaustion is deeper than I can fight, and I sink into sleep before I can beg for more.

CHAPTER TWENTY

URIEN

Placing a hand on Kari's leg, I feel her vibrations to check for any kind of injury. I've done so several times since she fell asleep, and she's fine. But another part of me can't understand that. She exploded like a star, and even for a fae, that much power should have killed or left some kind of permanent damage.

Though we don't know what kind of mark this will leave on her mind.

She has no idea how graceful she is. Watching her protect herself was what I hope watching her dance was like. Lithe and graceful and full of confident power. But after that...that was nothing like I've ever seen.

"Do we have a plan?" Verys asks softly.

Aeric nods, keeping his voice low. Kari is deeply asleep, and I don't think that anything we do will wake her, but we're all going to be careful anyway. "The beginnings of one. The Rialoir and Rialoia of the Crystal Court have once again agreed to help us."

I already knew this. Aeric asked me to help

approach them, as a Tiarne, which I was happy to do. I was more than a little surprised by their enthusiastic answer. "They've taken quite an interest in the human woman who's bound to Allwyn. Especially given the revelation of our relationship. Plus, Kaya speaks highly of Kari, and she is a valued member of their Court."

Verys crosses his arms. "How are they helping?"

"Location," I answer before Aeric. "You already know, but there are locations in the Crystal Court which are very isolated. They have several estates throughout the land and have offered them as places to spring the trap."

"They know there's a chance that they'll be destroyed?" Brae asks. He's been out looking for more information about Ariana and isn't quite up to speed.

"Yes," I say, leaning back against the wall and crossing my arms to keep from checking Kari again. "They didn't seem concerned. The idea that a fae would target anyone so blatantly—especially a human—is deeply offensive to them. They want to help."

Kent clears his throat softly. "I'm aware that I don't know everything about Fae politics. Why are we not asking the Rialoia of our own Court to help?"

I smile. I like that he's referring to the Carnal

Court as *our* Court. "Mostly timing," I say. "You all had already secured the help and hospitality of the Crystal Court. They did not need to have the whole situation broken down for them. But there's also the matter that we have brought danger into our Court and did not inform the Rialoia. I would much rather go to her and tell her that the threat has been neutralized than explain that we're setting a trap for a very dangerous fae inside our borders. And lastly, for obvious reasons the Carnal Court is always more populated with visitors than other Courts. This way there's less of a chance of any bystanders getting hurt. I don't think Ariana would hesitate to use that to her advantage."

"You're definitely correct on that one," Kent says.

Verys paces the length of the room and back. "Even with what we just saw, and the training we've done, is there any chance we'll convince her not to offer herself as bait?"

"I wish," I say. "But she has a point. Is there another way?"

"If there was another way, you'd be the one to find it," Brae points out, slowly moving away from Kari so he can stand and stretch.

He's right. I'm the diplomat, and not always by choice. We've all seen first-hand that violence leads to more violence. But in this case the fae we're dealing with isn't exactly going to sit down and have a heart to heart about what she wants. She's going to keep coming at us until we do something. This is that something.

"My main concern is what happens after," Verys says.

"After what?" Kent says.

"After we spring the trap. What's our aim? To catch her, find out what she wants, and then let her go?"

I shake my head. "No. We'll turn her over to the Crystal Court. The crimes she committed on their soil are more than enough to condemn her. And I daresay the Rialoia is eager to mete out justice, especially after hearing the full remainder of the story."

"Maybe she'll need a helping hand," Aeric mutters, stroking his hand down Kari's back.

Her hand is curled gently into his shirt, hair wildly spread and hiding her face. She's sweet, even in sleep. "The only question is now, how do we lead Ariana where we want her to go?"

"I suspect that we already have," Brae says.

Kent's eyebrows rise to his hairline. "What?"

"The magic," Verys says.

"Right." Brae leans closer to Kent so he doesn't have to speak as loudly. "The magic that she let go… that was not just simple magic. A blast like that would have been felt Courts away. Ariana has her ear to the ground. She is *looking* for Kari. If she doesn't know that we're here already, then she will soon."

Kent's hands still. He's been rubbing Kari's ankles and feet slowly. But now he's just looking at her. "Should we be getting ready to leave?"

"Soon," I say. "But I think we're all right for the night."

Verys nods in agreement. "We'll leave tomorrow, go home for a day. And when we go to the location we've chosen, we won't use any decoys. Blast it from the rooftops that that's where we're going."

"I don't like it," Kent says.

Aeric shakes his head and pulls Kari a little closer. "You and me both."

"We don't have a choice. Whatever she's planning, we need to know why she's coming after Kari so desperately. And if she's going to go after anyone else. We can't stop a plan that we don't know is in motion. We need this."

Brae rolls his eyes and chuckles, breaking the tension in the room. "We're not at Court, Urien. You can relax."

Verys smirks, and Kent covers his mouth with his hand. I sigh. I slip into the way I talk at Court a little too often. When you're there you usually have to convince people who aren't on your side to get on your side. And that sometimes means hammering a point home that they're already familiar with. "All right, asshole," I say. "I'm still right."

"Yes you are," Brae agrees. "Let's just hope all of this goes to plan."

I reach out to touch Kari one more time. Everything echoes just fine with my magic. She's all right. Yes, this needs to go to plan. For all our sakes.

CHAPTER TWENTY-ONE

KARI

I've had this dream before. Warmth in darkness and smooth touch. The echoes of unfamiliar magic. This time it's different. I can move, just a little, and when I open my mouth I can hear my voice. Though the sound is muffled like I'm underwater. "Who are you?"

The echo comes back just like last time, only stronger now. "Who are *you*?"

Lips find mine in the darkness. A taste of salt and rock and wind before the sadness hits and he's leaving. "Wait," I say. But he's already gone.

I wake with a start, but I'm not alone like I was the last time that I woke up from the dream. No, Aeric is holding me this time. And another body is pressed against my back—Urien.

"Good morning." That's Verys's voice from where he sits across the room.

"Morning," I whisper.

I should have known that even my quietest voice would be enough to wake the men next to me. Aeric groans with sleep, and rolls over me lazily. "It is morning. But I can think of a way to make it a truly *good* one."

Oh. I don't even have to tell him yes. He feels the way my breath hitches and the way I let my hips relax and legs slide apart. He chuckles. "I thought you might agree."

"I do."

Urien turns my face to his and kisses me, momentarily distracting me from the way Aeric is moving down my body with sinful intention. I keep my eyes open for a moment. Urien's eyes are gold with silver flecks like stars, and up close they look like galaxies. They're luminous set against the inky darkness of his skin, and I think I could just stare at them for a while.

But his tongue drifts along the seam of my lips and when I open for him he erases any thought of simply staring. He teases me with his own tongue in a way that foreshadows what's about to happen down below, as Aeric's hands deftly undo the buttons on my pants.

There's a brush of cool mint and spices before his tongue touches me, but just barely. And *Goddess* he doesn't even need his power to make every moment of this magic. I was already damp, but I grow wet under his tongue, and he groans, licking deeper and faster. *Fuck.*

The door opens, revealing Brae and Kent, who pause for a brief second before entering quickly and shutting the door. "If I'd known that Kari was an option, I would not have eaten breakfast."

"Too bad," Aeric says against my skin. "I thought of it first."

"I'm pretty sure I did," Brae says, laughing. "But Kari was still asleep."

The thought of waking up with Brae's clever tongue between my legs makes me shudder in anticipation and a new rush of wetness outwards. Aeric notices, and slowly seals his mouth over me while still meeting my eyes, showing me how much he likes my taste—so much that he'll drink it. My voice is half a moan when I speak. "You all have my permission to wake me up with your mouths any time you like."

The air in the room is suddenly charged with more sexual energy than it was before. "I'll remember that," Brae says softly.

Urien has lifted my shirt and bra, now teasing my nipples as Aeric teases my clit, and I can't find the words to say anything else. Everything is bliss.

They take their time. Lazy and tantalizing. I'm on the slow part of the rollercoaster, being pulled up with agonizing slowness towards a drop that is going to steal my breath and probably make me scream. I reach for Aeric's hair to pull him closer and this time he doesn't grab my wrists. He lets me sink my fingers into it, hair so dark you can just barely see the green sheen of it in the early light. He lets me pull his mouth harder against my clit, asking wordlessly for him to send me over.

But he doesn't right away. He builds. Sucks my clit between his lips and rolls it through before licking lower and plunging his tongue deep inside my pussy. It's such an intimate feeling, and one that never fails to take me by surprise. I moan, but it's caught by Urien's lips as he kisses my mouth again.

As Aeric fucks me with his tongue, he drags his thumb over my clit in circles. Matching those circles inside me, and everything goes from being delicious to white hot bright. I'm shaking under his lips, trying to reach that moment where everything falls away. One tiny stroke of magic from his tongue, and I'm gone. I cry out into Urien's mouth, and again as squeezes my nipples between his fingers, adding to everything falling into place and falling apart again.

A perfect, dizzying, spiral of power and pleasure.

I fall back into my body with one breath, and in the next I'm ready for more. Aeric could fuck me, and I'd be happy with that, but Kent steps up with a glint in his eyes. "Breakfast or not, I think I need a taste."

His eyes light me on fire, and I'm wet all over again. Brae comes to my side and leans down, taking a kiss that's less of a kiss and more of a statement of how deeply he wants and loves me.

Kent slides his hands up my clothed thighs, and I can feel his breath on my skin. I'm too lost in this kiss to realize what the sound is. And then I feel that the room has gone cold.

The door to the bedroom is standing open, Darran filling the frame with a face like thunder. His eyes take in the scene in front of him, and I'm so shocked that it takes me a moment to scramble to my senses and sit up, rearranging my clothing so I'm no longer exposed. This is not the Carnal Court, and we are not in public.

Darran's gaze is fixed on Verys. "You dare to invade my home under false pretenses of hospitality and then invite strangers?"

All the oxygen in the room is gone, and I swear the temperature has dropped so quickly that I'm shivering. Or maybe that's the adrenaline. My shield forms itself almost of it's own will, and I move it out so that it's also covering Verys. Like hell if Darran is going to lay a hand on him.

Verys knows what I've done, and he moves. Standing slowly, he deliberately steps outside the bound of my power. When I try to cover him with it again, his silvery power whips against mine sharply. A warning to stay back. And not protect him.

"My pretenses were not false. And I have not invited strangers. We share a mate. These are my brothers."

The look of disgust on Darran's face sends ice flooding through my veins. He looks at every one of the men and at me last. "I will not have this place turned into one of your Carnal whore houses. Bad enough that you've been fucking her like your life depended on it and degrading yourself by touching a human. This is beyond even what I imagined. It seems I was right about you, Verys."

Fury, clear and perfect, rolls through my chest. I take a step forward because I *am* going to punch him in the fucking face, when Brae's hand lands on my shoulder, gently pulling me back to his body. "Let him, Kari." The words are so soft that I'm the only one that can hear them. Just a breath at my ear.

Verys has lived with this man's hatred for more years than I can imagine. I don't want him to anymore. But he doesn't say anything immediately, just tilts his head slightly and examines the man who raised him.

Darran sneers. "Even after all this time, you're exactly the same. Not worth anything."

"I wonder what happened to the man who used

to tell me that I was the most promising warrior he'd ever seen," Verys says flatly.

"I never said that."

"On the contrary," Verys replies. "You said it nearly every day you saw me training. But that was when you thought I was your son. And no son of another man could be worth anything to you."

Power is coalescing inside Darran because of his fury. His hands ball into fists and I can feel his rage seething from here. "You're still a child, and one of betrayal. Nothing but a *maerach*." He spits the word at Verys, and though I don't know what it means, I can feel the hatred ringing through it. "It would have been better for Allwyn to strip you of your magic entirely and let you fade."

Verys just sighs. "What you're asking is to erase myself from existence because the world didn't bend itself to your will, and I can't do that. I can't apologize for my existence either, though you know that I've tried. It's not my fault that my mother found love, and it was not with you.

"We will leave immediately, because in spite of your treatment of her and me, I still love Siona. I do not want there to be any repercussions for her if you revoke her hospitality." He takes a step forward then. "But make no mistake, Darran. If you insult my mate or my Court again, or if you attempt to harm Siona as retribution for my actions, you will be accountable to the Goddess. I will make sure of it."

The low, calm tone of his words make them cut deeper. Darran stares at him, and the room feels breathless. I don't think Verys has ever spoken to him this way before, and he was not expecting it. "Leave," Verys says. "When you return home in one hour, we will be gone."

Darran straightens and sends a final, poisonous glance throughout the room. "See that you are." The door slams behind him as he leaves.

"Verys," I say, stepping towards him.

He shakes his head. "Get her home. I must speak to Siona before I join you."

I ignore his protest and wrap my arms around him. "I know that was difficult."

"Yes," he says, kissing the top of my head. "But it was necessary." He leaves the room without fanfare, and it takes only a few moments to gather the things we've brought and step through a portal back home. Finally, even if just for a little while, I'm home.

CHAPTER TWENTY-TWO

VERYS

I find my mother in the kitchen, and she knows something is wrong immediately. "I have to leave."

"Why?" Her eyes go wide. But when she sees my expression, "Darran."

"He is gone for the moment, but he will not be pleased when he comes back. I told him what I truly thought of him. It wasn't the easiest conversation."

She chuckles. "No, I imagine not."

"We're leaving. Things are moving and we can't stay, and I don't want to make things worse."

I notice the way her scars move when she smiles at me, and she reaches up to place a hand on my cheek. "Nothing you have ever done has made things worse, Verys. I chose this. I must live with the consequences."

Wrapping her in my arms, I truly hug her for the first time since I arrived. She feels smaller than I remember. Perhaps because it's been so long, and perhaps because she has withered under Darran's gaze. "I will come back," I say. "I will come to the

Court to see you. I'm sorry that I stayed away so long."

"Don't you dare do it again," she says. "And when you return, bring Kari with you. She's lovely, and I would still like to know my new daughter."

Her words take my breath, and suddenly I'm fighting unexpected emotion. She embraces me again. "The Goddess has placed you on this path," she says. "See it through to the end."

"I will."

She pulls herself back gently. "Now go. He will not be far, and your mate has already left. No doubt he will return sooner than you expect."

"I'm sorry, Mother."

She shakes her head. "Never be sorry. Not for this."

There is nothing left to say, and I cut a portal back to the Carnal Court through the air. I step through it, and as I look back Siona waves her hand in farewell. Exactly as she said I see Darran stalk into the room as the portal is closing, equal measures of satisfaction and fury on his face. He got what he wanted—me gone. My one consolation is that the vows my mother swore to him protect her too. He cannot cause her true harm when she is bound to him the way she is. It would cause him pain, and if there's one thing Darran cannot stand it is his own pain.

I'm standing in the entry to the mansion at home, the wards pulsing behind me. This is where I'm meant to be. I've never felt that underlying sense of *rightness* that I felt as a child in the Lunar Court. Not until now, anyway. I've embraced the magic, and so in return the Court has embraced me.

When Darran burst into that room, I felt my heart drop into my feet. I expected everything that he said and more. It's nothing that he hasn't already said to me in the past. But seeing the way he looked at Kari, at the other men, I felt power and fire that I never have before. I used to crave Darran's forgiveness, and thought that simply letting him do as he wished might make him see that I was not the monster that he made me out to be. But you cannot argue with a person like that.

He has long since made up his mind what to think of me, and I can live with that. But I will not stand by while he hurls abuse at my family. My *mate*.

Everything in my mind was so clear in that moment, and it feels good. Like a long overdue relief from a weight that's been sitting on my shoulders. I feel truly whole for the first time in recent memory. Thank the Goddess.

Everyone is in the main living area when I enter the house, talking quickly. "What's happening?"

Kari launches herself off the couch at me, and I catch her in my arms. Her arms are locked around my neck, and the worry is bleeding off of her like rain. "I'm fine," I whisper. "Better than fine."

"I'm so proud of you. But is Siona all right?"

"She will be for the moment. We'll be going back to see her soon enough, without Darran."

She buries her face in my neck. "Good."

I kiss her hair, inhaling the floral scent of her. Every time I hold her in my arms I can't believe that she's mine. Over her shoulder, I glance at the others and raise my eyebrows.

"Kari's...explosion yesterday was felt here," Brae says.

That's further than I even thought possible. "People are asking questions?"

"Yes," Urien says.

Aeric is calmly sharpening one of his most vicious knives. So there's no doubt that Ariana knows. If we're going to spring the trap, it has to be soon. It's to our benefit that she thinks that we're panicked and hiding Kari from being exposed with so much magic."

I look to Urien again, who's leaning against a

column with a massive sword strapped to his back. "The Rialoi? They are informed?"

"They are."

"What's stopping us then?" I ask.

Kari is the one who speaks. "We were waiting for you. And also I'm nervous."

Setting her on her feet so I can look into her eyes, I brush back her hair. "You can do this. Anything is within your grasp, and we will not be far away. You only have to hold on long enough for us to get there. That's all."

She takes a deep breath in, and I see the confidence that my words hold take root. "Okay."

"I'd rather do this sooner than later," Brae says. "The faster we get there, the sooner it is over."

"Agreed." I'll be happy to put this episode behind us where it belongs. I look down at Kari. "Are you ready?"

She nods. "Got armor and everything."

"Then let's go," Aeric says. "Verys, grab your weapons. We'll get the portal."

CHAPTER TWENTY-THREE

KARI

The place that they've chosen to set this trap is stunning. A mansion fit for the Rialoi that occasionally occupy it, it's a perfect example of the beauty of the Crystal Court. The entire mansion is formed from what looks like wood, but it is carved to mimic it. The amount of craftsmanship is truly stunning.

When we arrived through the portal, the guys fanned out and checked every crevice of the building, and I tried to help, expanding my magic to feel for anything out of place. But there's nothing. If we weren't here for a very specific purpose, I could spend hours exploring this place and looking at the intricate carvings and inventive furnishings that have been created from every kind of crystal.

As it is, I've settled myself in the gargantuan main hall, where an emerald chandelier overhangs a table formed of one large black and white agate. The fireplace at the end of the room keeps things bright and warm as the light fades. I'm alone here now, the men having fallen back to positions far enough away that they'll be able to hear me scream, but not so close that Ariana will be able to sense them when she comes. It's going to be a delicate balance of my holding out against her and giving them enough time to arrive.

They hate this as much as I do. The way they kissed me hard before they closed the door behind them is proof enough of that, but no one said it. We can't think about the possibility of failure. We're already all nervous enough.

I don't know how long it will take for Ariana to arrive. We portaled very publicly in front of the mansion and outside the wards so that she would know where we were going. But she is smart and has been one step ahead of us. She may take her time. But I don't sit, choosing to walk small circles, clockwise and counter, around the table. I don't want to be caught off-guard. Never again.

My shield glitters visibly around me, power continually flowing to it from me. I barely have to think about it now, but I still do my best to concentrate and to keep it strong.

Hours pass. I have to rebuild the fire more than once, and by the time the bright is starting to lighten the sky again, my eyes are gritty with lack of sleep and I'm yawning. It's been truly a long time since I've pulled an all-nighter, and I'm not a nineteen-year-old college student anymore. I'm not built to be awake for more than a day at a time.

The caress of magic is so soft against the shield, that I almost miss it. It's gentle and testing. Barely a brush, but it's there. I only have time to look in that direction before the force of the wave hits me and knocks me sideways. The shield is up, but barely. I pour more power into it and get to my feet, staring into the darkness.

That's not Ariana.

A sharp smile forms in the darkness, and my heart leaps into my throat and stays there. It's *him*. The fae male that attacked me. My sixth mate. He's dressed entirely in black, fitted pants and a shirt that make him look like night incarnate with his dark hair and eyes. Blue-tinged power rolls at his fingertips, sharpening and lengthen into something wicked. "Hello, Kari," he says. That voice is resonant. It echoes off the walls of the room and vibrates through my chest.

My body responds to him even though I don't want it to. My soul knows him, knows he's *mine* and wants to hear that voice when it's in the throes of passion and commanding my pleasure. Not trying to kill me. But he *is* trying to kill me. Focus, Kari. "What's your name? Since we keep meeting like this."

He makes a mock bow. "Kiaran, at your service."

Kiaran. I roll his name through my mind. Why has Allwyn bound me to him like this? The goddess said that both she and the land make decisions that are in the best interest of Allwyn and it's people. Always. "Ariana?" I ask.

"Sends her regards, but you'll see her soon."

I swallow, to try to keep him talking. "Too afraid to come herself?"

One side of his mouth tips up into a vicious grin, and he begins to circle me. I move in the opposite direction maintaining our distance from each other. "Too smart to fall for your little trap. She knows your precious men would never leave you alone on purpose."

"So she sends her guard dog to kill me?"

"That would be easier," he says. "But no. Ariana wants you alive."

"Why?"

He shakes his head. "You'll have to ask her." And then he lunges. The spears of his power collide with my shield at the same moment I throw a blast of power out towards him. The force of his magic nearly makes me drop to my knees. I should have thought of this. Should have remembered. This is the fae who ensnared four of my mates with his magic and still had enough power to move and fight. My skill isn't a good match for this.

Another meteoric crash of blue fire whips around me, and I feel for a moment like I'm underwater in an infinite sea, and the recognition makes me lose my focus. The dreams are him. He and I together, if only for a moment. That's his magic that I felt and wanted more of. I had thought that it was just a dream. Something my brain made up. Echoes of all the magic flinging itself around inside me.

No.

I was dreaming of—longing for—my mate.

Goddess, why?

Power rushes up through me and out, barely managing to blunt the edge of his next attack. "You're not doing a very good job of making me think that you don't want to kill me."

"I can't take you if I can't get to you," he says, smirking, though he's breathing as hard as I am. "That's an impressive shield for a human."

The moments he's standing still and talking are a blessing. I reach for more magic, letting it fill my fingers and bolster my protection. He sees it and slowly shakes his head.

"It would be easier, Kari, if you just gave up. I'm going to take you, no matter how long it takes to wear down that magic. We could save ourselves some time and just give in."

"So you can deliver me to a madwoman intent on

torturing me and using me for Goddess knows what? No thanks, I'll pass."

Can the fae men feel the magic that's happening in here? Why haven't they come? I scream at the top of my lungs. I can hold out, but not forever. Not against this kind of battering ram.

Kiaran narrows his eyes. "Close enough to hear your call? Figures. But they won't be a problem, I'm sure." He jumps, driving a wedge of power down into the shield above me, and I feel it in my chest. *Fuck.* "What did you do?" I ask, voice rasping with the effort.

"Did you think that Ariana would send me alone?" Another crack of power directly down on my head, and I stumble, struggling to fill in the fissures he's making in the shield. Are they all right? Are they fighting? I can't breathe, realizing that one of them might be dying and I would not know it. If I had sealed my bonds with them, hadn't been so afraid of it, I'd know if they were in trouble and they would know what's happening here.

In one heartbeat I've made the decision that if I make it out of here, I'm sealing the bonds. All of them. When it feels right. But I don't want to feel like this ever again.

Kiaran's magic slips over my shield, completely encircling it. Every inch of it is covered like a glove, and it squeezes like a boa constrictor. I push back, but it feels like I'm drowning in it. "Please don't do this," I say, backing away, hoping some physical distance between us will help. It doesn't. He's not going to hurt me. He needs to deliver me. All he needs to do is wear me down. One crack, and it's finished.

I call out again, hoping that they'll hear me. But my voice echoes off the walls of Kiaran's power. When he speaks it's just slightly muffled—the way he and I sound in our dream—like he's underwater. "That's enough, Kari." The magic constricts, and I give in just a touch, bring the shield closer to my body.

"No." Stretching my arms out to either side, I start to pray. *Please please please please. Help.*

But the answer isn't the one I hope to hear. It's the voice I've heard before, with the same message.

Choose.

Choose what? I beg.

Choose.

Kiaran is holding his hands in front of him like he's got a ball between them, fingers outstretched, and I watch as he compressed them, and the force of his magic grows, squeezing my shield even smaller. And smaller still. I reach down into the depths of this golden spring inside me, and I unleash the power. The shield expands for a moment, and I know that I can break through it. I can blast him away from me. I can escape. But I can feel the amount of power in my hands, and as my awareness expands, I can feel him just the way I felt the others on the mountain side.

He will not see it coming—does not imagine that I contain the multitudes of magic that I do. I can release this power now, and I will win. But he will die.

Choose.

Familiar fury rises in my chest. *How can you ask me to do this?*

I can still try to hold out. There's nothing saying that I have to give in. But I have to make this choice. Fight back or hold on. It's another knot in the strings, infinite possibilities branching forward. Twisting away from me and waiting for me in this moment.

I'm sorry. That last is not to the goddess. It's to my mates fighting outside who don't know. I swallow the power back down, funneling it into my shrinking shield, and Kiaran smiles. He felt the power, and he felt me give it up, and thinks that I'm letting go. He has no idea.

"You could have made this easy," he says, crushing his hands together.

My shield shatters under the force of his magic, and I'm driven to the ground with the force of the blow. Instantly, he's on me, hand at my throat, face close to mine. That face is twisted in ugly victory, and then it's not. The moment his hand touches my skin he hisses in pain and flinches back.

His face changes. The evil taint in his eye falls away, and he nearly collapses on top of me. He's holding his hand, and when he pulls himself upright, cradling his hand, he looks like a completely different person. "No," he whispers, looking at me in horror. "No, you can't be."

He doesn't make a move to stop me as I scramble away from him. My power is back under my grasp, and I bring the shield back in full force. "What the fuck just happened? Why do you look different?"

"You're my mate."

I've never heard such anguish in a voice, and I can't lie. "Yes," I breathe.

"Please, no." I don't think he's speaking to me. "I'm so sorry, Kari."

"You didn't answer my question. What the *fuck* just happened?"

He shakes his head. "I don't have time to explain. Not fully. But her power—she is in control most of the time."

Touching me released him from whatever hold

she has on him. He stands and takes a step closer, and I take one back towards the wall. "I won't hurt you," he says, voice fervent.

"Yes, you would."

"Not if I truly have a choice." This time when he takes a step forward, I let him. To the edge of the shield. "And when she's there, I don't."

"Do you know why she wants me?"

"She needs your power," he says quickly, hands shaking at his sides. "Especially now that she's realized that you have more than she thought. Magic that isn't yours. She was just going to kill you—a loose end. But you're more valuable alive."

"Why?"

He shakes his head and tries to approach but the shield holds him back. "She hasn't told me. Or if she has I don't remember, but she's not going to stop. She will go to any length, Kari."

We're at a stand still, and he's blocked away from me. Slowly, he places a hand on the barrier, and I reach out with my power. I feel no threat from him right now. "I want to touch you," he says. "Just once."

There's the echo of the Goddess's voice in my head. *Choose.*

Slowly, I let him through, and he crosses the distance between us. He's beautiful. Dark and brooding, all sharp angles and the scent of water. He reaches out with his fingertips to brush my cheek, and again he hisses in obvious pain at contact with my skin.

But that doesn't stop him as he reaches out and pulls me into a furious kiss. He groans in pain, but to me this is anything but pain. This feels like a brand on my soul. Now that I know the taste of his lips and the wash of pure blue magic over me, I'll never be able to forget it.

Kissing him feels like taking the first breath after surfacing from being under the ocean too long. It feels like breathing even though he's stealing my breath. His fingers tangle in my hair, gripping it to the point of pain, and he pulls away with a moan. "I hurt you," I say.

"Yes."

"Why?"

"I thought my mate was another," he says, and the raw grief on his face is something I won't be able to unsee. Suddenly he goes stiff, and then his body relaxes. I see the change in his face, though it's not complete.

"She's coming back?"

"Yes." He nods, forcing the word out, hand growing even tighter in my scalp, and I can't breathe.

I lift my chin and look him in the eye, focusing on the deep blue color and not on the way his body is pressed against mine, cradled perfectly. "Kiaran. Do you want to hurt me?"

His lips fall on mine again with bruising force, and we crash into the wall together. I'm pinned by him, raw force holding me in place but also holding him back. "This magic—" he falters. "Yes, I want to hurt you." There's conflict there. The magic that's taken hold of his brain telling him the only way to find satisfaction is to cause me harm. He's warring with himself, even as he kisses my jaw with desperation.

Kiaran rips himself away from me, his lips red as though he's been burned from kissing my skin, and he looks at me. "She will never stop," he says. "Never."

Before I can say another word, his body goes rigid, face contorted with pain before he almost throws himself out the door of the mansion. The magic overtook him again, and I wonder what it cost him to leave without taking me with him.

Goddess.

I sag against the wall, the fight draining out of me. That choice, I made the right one. But how do I explain this? How do I tell them what happened?

"Kari!" I hear the shout from far away. It's not just a shout, it's a warning. My senses pick it up a second later—the danger. Across the room the fire spins out of control, suddenly a bonfire that's unable to be contained. Real and vicious magic tears through the house, and this time it tastes of her. Orange and ash, burnt and dead things. More than I've ever felt before. It's tearing the house apart, and I can't move. Gravity suddenly seems thick like syrup and my limbs will not obey. The only thing I have is power.

And now, I unleash everything.

Light blazes around me like a star as the building falls around me. Thousands of pounds of stone and crystal crack into pieces and cascade onto the ground. But not on me. They melt into glass in the heat of this sparkling fury, and I let everything pour out. Pain and rage and frustration and grief for my mate who currently is in pain. Anger that I had to choose, and relief that I chose correctly.

The building disintegrates into sand around me, and if I hadn't had the shield of this magic, I would be crushed beneath it. I can see my mates running towards me, more than one bloodied and broken as I let the magic go, and succumb to the sudden exhaustion of releasing everything.

Arms catch me before the world goes black.

CHAPTER TWENTY-FOUR

KARI

"Kari," the muffled voice says, reaching out with an aching sweep of blue power. "Kari."

The voice is sad, and I want to comfort him, but when I reach out, he's not there. I can't feel him. "I'm here."

Kari. It's barely a whisper now. Filled with longing.

When I open my eyes there are tears on my cheeks. I turn my face into my pillow and let the sob escape me. Kiaran. His pain echoes in my chest, and there's nothing that I can do about it. Not now. Not until I figure out exactly how to free him. And I will. No matter what it takes, I will make sure my mate is released from Ariana and her power.

"Kari?" Verys's voice sounds from the doorway, and then he's by my side.

"Bad dream," I mutter, as the rest of my mates enter and sit. "Are you guys all right? You were ambushed."

"How did you know?" Brae asks. There's a nasty

bruise on his face and Urien has a cut on his arm that's nearly healed. Probably due to his talent.

I stretch, realizing I'm still in the clothes I wore, and I'm covered in glass dust. "Aside from the way you look? Kiaran told me."

Aeric snaps to attention. "Kiaran?"

"The fae who attacked Verys," I say. "He was there instead of Ariana."

Kent curses under his breath.

"She wants my power, he doesn't know why, but he said that she's not going to stop. Ever."

Brae shakes his head and reaches to stroke down my leg. "Why would he tell you that?"

My voice catches in my throat. How do I explain? "The power controlling him—it broke. He was free. But only for a moment. He chose to tell me those things and leave."

"That makes sense," Verys says. "Given what we've seen. The people who attacked us seemed to be controlled, and I imagined the people that brought down the building were as well. Kiaran leaving the building must have been a signal. They didn't make it."

Sadness hits me in a rush. To Ariana, those fae were expendable. But they were fae with lives, and families. Who knows how they got mixed up with her, but they don't deserve that. "Will you be able to find out where they're from."

"I can do that," Brae says. "And if I can't, I can give them the proper rites."

"Good." I lean against Verys. We all take a moment of silence, not consciously, just letting the sadness breathe. They haven't told me much about their time in the war, but I hope that I'm doing this right. I will acknowledge sadness and death, but I refuse to let it dictate me. I want to live, and love, and be free. "I know we have to make a new plan, but Ariana does as well. Can we take a day to breathe?"

Urien smiles. "I think that can be arranged. What did you have in mind?"

"I can think of some unfinished business from yesterday," Kent says, chuckling.

"Actually," I say, "Though I'm looking forward to that unfinished business a *lot*, Verys and I have some unfinished business of our own."

He looks down at me, surprised. "We do?"

"We do."

Urien laughs. "Have fun."

I roll off the bed and grab Verys's hand. I've already told the house exactly what I need, and I pull him into his room. He's smiling as I push him onto the bed. "Not that I'm complaining about what's about to happen, but after a week spent nearly alone, what kind of unfinished business do we have?"

I straddle his waist and kiss him, enjoying the feeling of him growing hard underneath me. "You gave me your firsts," I say. "Almost all of them. I want to return the favor."

Confusion crosses his face, and then clarity. His eyes go wide when I grab his hands and guide them to my ass. Over his shoulder I see the bottle of lubricant I asked the house to put here. Fuck I love magic. Verys's voice is hoarse with need. "Are you sure?"

"Yes," I breathe against his lips. "I want to do this. I want to be able to have you. And—" I cut off, blood rising to my cheeks. It's not easy to say out loud. "I want to be able to have more than one of you at once. This is the first step."

Silver eyes go dark in a haze of lust, and I swear that he's so hard he's about to burst out of his trousers. "Are you sure you don't want someone with more experience?"

"I want us to learn together," I say, pulling the dusty shirt over my head. "I asked the house to give us what we needed." He starts laughing when he sees the bottle, and grabs it as he strips down. I strip down too, crawling onto his bed.

When he turns back to me, I wiggle my ass at

him. "I'm so fucking lucky," he says. "To have you as a mate."

"Right back at you there."

Hands fall on my ass, stroking and smoothing down. Verys leans over me, kissing the nape of my neck and letting me feel the length of him pressed against my spine. Goddess, this is going to be something. Dragging his hand up the inside of my thigh, he teases me. Dipping his fingers into me before drawing circles around my clit, warming me up. Can't hurt.

Without warning, he slips his cock into my pussy and plunges deep. I nearly come right then. He holds my hips as he plunges in, using the long, steady strokes that I've come to crave from him. The orgasm rolls in like a tide, filling me up slowly, building to a crescendo, and then nothing. He pulls back only seconds before I'm about to go over and I groan in frustration. "What the fuck? Oohhh—"

Cold lubricant spreads over my ass, and I understand. He's taken me to the edge of pleasure so that I'm already blissed out on his cock. Leaning over me again, he kisses the edge of my ear. "Are you sure?"

"Yes." I arch my ass up into him. "You want this ass?"

"Fuck, Kari," he says. "You have no idea."

"Then take it."

One hand lands on my lower back, steadying me as he lines up, and I feel him against me, slowly pushing. Goddess, he feels so much bigger when he's pressing in here. I don't know if he's going to fit. Is it even possible? My breath goes short as he pushes further, and I force my body to relax. Suddenly he slips past the tightest part, and he's in. He curses and I do too. Fuck it feels so strange, and amazing. There's a small amount of pain too, but nothing like what I thought it might be.

Every other part of me feels so sensitive now, from my skin down to my clit. Like they're suddenly on alert because this is a sensation that they've never felt before. He sinks in a little deeper and I swear that I see stars. Adding magic to his gentle thrusts only makes it better. I've got sensations zinging through me that I never imagined that I would have, and it's un-fucking-believable.

"You have no idea how good this feels," he says, sinking in further.

My voice is more moan than words. "I think I have a pretty good idea."

When he's so deep in me that I don't think I can possibly take any more, he's still plunging further. My fingers grip the bedsheets like a vice just for something, anything to hold on to. I'm panting, desperate, wanting. Verys pulls back, the reverse friction driving me mad, and I can't hold myself back any longer. I come, ecstasy making me go blind with sensation. I bear down on his cock, and Verys nearly collapses on top of me. "Fuck, Kari."

"Yes, please," I manage to say.

Laughing, he takes the hint, plunging in again just to pull back and fuck deeper. I've barely finished the first orgasm when the second one hits, bigger than the last. It's an earthquake inside of me, pulling apart fault lines I've never felt. My clit is so sensitive and swollen that it's aching, begging to be touched, and I think I might actually beg.

Verys hand slips around my legs and strokes me there, and I come again. "Verys!" His name echoes off the walls and I collapse onto the bed, unable to hold myself up any longer as he takes me deeper. He's close himself grunting with every thrust, pounding faster and faster until he cries out, releasing heat inside me. Just that sends off aftershocks in my belly, making me shake helplessly as he spends himself inside me.

I don't know why I waited so long to do that. If I'd known it would be that good I would have added that to my list of party tricks years ago. "Amazing," I say, as he pulls out of me, covering my body with his and kissing down my spine.

"Yes." His voice is reverent. "Thank you for sharing that with me."

I roll over underneath him and lift my mouth to his. "I love you."

"And I you." His forehead presses against mine. "I'm grateful for unfinished business."

I laugh. "Me too."

At least, I am in this context. There's so much more unfinished business than I want to think about. Kiaran and Ariana. Whatever she's trying to accomplish by taking magic. Sealing the mating bonds and building a life here. So many things to figure out that it's overwhelming. But I can take the day to breathe. Just one day, and then I'll start to figure out what the hell to do. And I'll have help.

Verys pulls me into his arms and lifts me off the bed. "Where are we going?"

"We're not the only ones with unfinished business," he says, dragging his lips across my neck, leaving a trail of delicious heat.

I laugh as he carries me back into my bedroom, where the guys are still sitting, and places me on the bed like an offering. "Kent," he says. "Unfinished business?"

"Absolutely." Kent strips off his shirt and leans down to kiss me.

There's laughter and fire and pleasure in this

room, and through it all, I have a bolt of fear. This is all too perfect. It's what I want every day for the rest of my life. But I can't quite let go of that thread of terror running underneath it all. Because deep in my mind, I can still hear that lingering, echoing voice.

Choose.

To be continued...

Want to know what happens next? Aeric, Brae, Kent, Verys, Urien, and Kiaran are waiting for you in *Shameless*.

KEEP IN TOUCH!

Devyn's Newsletter:

Be the first to hear updates about my new releases, sexy exclusive content, and the occasional dessert recipe!

https://www.subscribepage.com/devynsinclair

Devyn's Facebook Group:

Come hang out with us! We talk about books —*especially* the sexy ones—share memes and hot inspiration photos and more!

https://www.facebook.com/groups/devynsinclair/

ABOUT THE AUTHOR

Devyn Sinclair writes steamy Reverse Harem romances for your wildest fantasies. Every sexy story is packed with the right amount steam, hot men, and delicious happy endings.

She lives in the wilds of Montana in a small red house with a crazy orange cat. When Devyn's not writing, she spends time outside in big sky country, continues her quest to find the best lemon pastry there is, and buys too many books. (Of course!)

To connect with Devyn:

ALSO BY DEVYN SINCLAIR

The Carnal Court

* * *

Fevered

Euphoria

Shameless

Breathless

War of Heavenly Fire

Queen of Darkness

Queen of Torment

Queen of Annihilation

The Royal Celestials

The Virgin Queen

Printed in Great Britain
by Amazon